CLAIMING HIS MATE

A CRESCENT MOON STORY

Savannah Stuart

Copyright © 2013 by Savannah Stuart

All rights reserved. Except as permitted under the U.S. Copyright Act of 1976, no part of this publication may be reproduced, distributed, or transmitted in any form or by any means, or stored in a database or retrieval system, without the prior written permission of the author. Thank you for buying an authorized version of this book and complying with copyright laws. You're supporting writers and encouraging creativity.

Cover art: Jaycee of Sweet 'N Spicy Designs
Author website: www.savannahstuartauthor.com

Publisher's Note: This is a work of fiction. Names, characters, places, and incidents are either the products of the author's imagination or used fictitiously, and any resemblance to actual persons, living or dead, or business establishments, organizations or locales is completely coincidental.

Claiming His Mate/KR Press, LLC -- 1st ed.
ISBN-10: 1942447094
ISBN-13: 9781942447092

Praise for the books of Savannah Stuart

"Fans of sexy paranormal romance should definitely treat themselves to this sexy & fun story." —Nina's Literary Escape

"I enjoyed this installment so much I'll be picking up book one...worth the price for the punch of plot and heat."
—Jessie, HEA USA Today blog

"...a scorching hot read." —The Jeep Diva

"This story was a fantastic summer read!" —Book Lovin' Mamas

"If you're looking for a hot, sweet read, be sure not to miss Tempting Alibi. It's one I know I'll revisit again and again."
—Happily Ever After Reviews

"You will not regret reading the previous story or this one. I would recommend it to anyone who loves a great shifter story."
—The Long & Short of It

"...a fun and sexy shapeshifter book and definitely worth the read."
—The Book Binge

CHAPTER ONE

Lauren Hayes shoved a wayward strand of hair under the knit cap she wore as she slid up to the outside back wall of the quiet, two-story house. The black cover over her hair had nothing to do with the chilly October weather. Right now she was all about blending into the shadows this cold fall night. Which meant dressing in all black, like a sneaky burglar.

Because she was about to do something stupid. Incredibly stupid. She inwardly berated herself.

There was no turning back now. Shifters were notorious gossips and word had spread through the grapevine that Grant Kincaid, alpha of the Kincaid wolf pack in Gulf Shores, Alabama was on a honeymoon.

With his new human mate.

That by itself had shocked the shifter world. Kincaid's father had been a brutal bastard—before he'd died. A shitty alpha who'd hated anyone who wasn't supernatural. Or at least that's what Lauren had heard.

The current alpha was two hundred years old and she was twenty-five so it wasn't as if they'd ever run in the same circles. She'd also heard Grant wasn't like his father and from the brief meeting she and her pride had with him six months ago, she had to agree that he seemed pretty decent.

Even if he was a stubborn ass who refused to give her family back what was rightfully theirs. Now that the alpha was out of town, she and some of her pridemates had decided to break into his house.

To steal from him.

Maybe steal was a bit of a stretch, she thought as she moved against the side of the house. Wind whipped around her, sending another shiver racing through her. She was simply taking back something that belonged to her family's pride. She had to remind herself of that. Her sister was getting married in two weeks and the broach the elder Kincaid had taken from her family almost a hundred years ago was supposed to have been a wedding gift when the oldest Hayes daughter got married. The piece of jewelry had been in their family for centuries. Well, the jewels had been. Three, four-carat—*colorless*—diamonds and a handful of emeralds had been passed down from oldest daughter to oldest daughter in some form of jewelry ever since. When Lauren's mother had received a necklace from her mother, she'd had the jewels put into a broach instead.

And Lauren desperately wanted to give it to her sister Stacia as a wedding gift. She deserved it.

Since Lauren was one of the few shifters on the planet who could mask their scent from other shifters, vampires and pretty much all supernatural beings, she'd been more or less volunteered for the job by her cousins. She also had a knack for breaking into places. Not that she was normally a thief. Her cousin Tommy, however, was. When she'd been twelve he'd taught her a lot of tricks, including picking locks and hotwiring cars. Her parents had been so pissed when they'd found out. After she stole back what was rightfully theirs, she bet they'd be glad she had those extra skills. Of course they'd be angry at her for doing this, but she'd known if she told them they would have ordered her not to. She figured it was better to do this then beg forgiveness later.

She had a few pridemates waiting a mile away in case she ran into trouble, but they had to stay out of sight unless she called them.

Right now they were all on Kincaid territory. Didn't matter that it was a touristy beach town right on the Gulf Coast and that humans had no idea a shifter pack had carved out an area to live here. As a jaguar shifter, she knew she shouldn't be here without permission so if she got caught she was so screwed. Wolves weren't known for being forgiving. And stealing from an alpha? She shoved those thoughts out of her head. If she was scared, she couldn't work.

Here goes nothing.

The two story house was raised like most houses on the beach but he also had an upstairs patio that she planned to use to her full advantage. She shimmied up one of the columns with a preternatural speed and hoisted herself up and over the lattice style barrier. Being a cat, she was nimble and quick on her feet, but it still took strength to do this in human form.

Crouching low to the ground, she carefully looked around the large patio at the closed French doors and then back at the beach. The waves sounded softly about a hundred yards away, the calm methodic rhythm doing little to soothe the nerves punching through her. She was about to break into an alpha's home. So, so, so stupid. But it would make her mother and sister happy.

Thankfully the quarter moon was hidden by clouds, further helping her cover. She'd been watching the Kincaid pack's comings and goings for the last week in preparation for tonight. It was midnight so almost every one of them was at one of the many bars or the hotel Kincaid owned. They all worked together as a big family. Their hours were more like vampires' than shifters', but clearly it worked for the pack because they were ridiculously wealthy.

Owning beach front property anywhere could be pricey, but they also owned an entire condominium building next door to Kincaid's personal residence. At least almost everyone was at work. And even though she knew for a fact they had a security system, she'd thrown a giant boulder through the back French doors a couple days ago in preparation.

Lauren had felt like a total jerk doing it, but she'd needed them to replace the doors. Which they'd done this morning. The chances of them having already replaced the security contact that would be standard with the system on the new doors was about five percent. More like zero percent considering she'd been watching the house practically ever since she'd ruined the doors. And when she hadn't been spying, one of her pridemates had.

As she examined the French doors now she realized the lock was also new. And it wasn't the cheap kind either. But, she was very good at getting into places she shouldn't.

Less than sixty seconds later she was inside the master bedroom. After a quick perusal of the top part of the door frame she breathed a sigh of relief to see no new contacts in place. Carefully closing the door behind her, she paused and glanced around the giant room. With her supernatural eyesight she didn't need to turn on a light to see everything—not that she would anyway. Might as well just put up a bright neon sign that she'd broken in.

The furniture was masculine, but there were definitely feminine touches. Not that Lauren cared about any of the décor. Now she was focused on looking for a safe. If he were going to hide diamonds and emeralds, it would definitely be in a safe. There was a slim chance he'd put it in a bank vault, but shifters and vamps, especially one as old as him, were weird about that stuff. No, they liked to keep their valuables close on hand.

For all she knew a silent alarm had gone off. There weren't any visible sensors in the bedroom, but that didn't mean shit. She knew that by breaking in blind without knowing the complete layout of the security system she was taking a chance but almost no one had sensors in their bedrooms. It didn't make sense. Living room areas and downstairs areas of course, but bedrooms and any upstairs saw too much foot traffic on a daily basis.

Moving quickly and quietly she went to the most obvious place to hide a safe. The closet. Nothing there. She searched behind picture frames next, then everywhere else she could think of before moving to the next room. The door was open to reveal an office.

Pausing, she could hear only the wind and waves outside. There were residual scents in the house but that made sense. She stepped inside the room, her boots silent against the rich hardwood floor. Two steps in, she realized she wasn't alone. It was like an abrupt assault on her senses and her inner animal simply knew.

Before she could turn fully around, she was tackled to the ground by a huge male. Definitely supernatural.

Strong, muscular arms encircled her from behind, throwing her to the ground, the male on top of her. Somehow he managed to angle their fall so he took the brunt of the impact on his arms. All the air left her lungs in a whoosh as panic slammed through her. She hadn't heard him, hadn't even scented him. That alone told her how dangerous he was.

Though all her animal instinct told her to fight, she knew she was at a disadvantage. Going limp, she didn't struggle. The second she was set free or her captor loosened his grip, she was running. Wolves might be strong, but jaguars were wicked fast. In human and shifter form.

"What the hell are you doing sneaking around in wolf territory in *my* alpha's fucking house?" a familiar male voice said near her ear, a trickle of his fresh scent that reminded her of the beach in winter enveloping her.

She hadn't scented him before, probably because of her own fear and panic at doing such a stupid thing—but now his scent covered her. She shivered at the sound of Max McCray's voice. Kincaid's second-in-command. He was supposed to be at the Crescent Moon Bar tonight working.

Lauren swallowed hard. "I want *my* family's fucking jewels back," she gritted out. There was no sense in lying. He'd be able to scent the bitter, acidic stench if she tried. She could normally cover her scent well, but right now she was nervous and couldn't keep her gift under control. Blind panic hummed through her, her inner jaguar telling her to run, run, *run*.

But she couldn't. Not with Max's massive body on top of her, keeping her pinned in place.

She was ashamed to admit that she'd had more than a handful of fantasies about the dark-haired, muscular shifter with the piercing blue eyes. None like this, with her flat on her stomach and him behind her... Okay, that was a lie. She'd had those types of fantasies too. Of course they'd both been naked and she hadn't been working as a thief.

"Such language," he murmured, his mouth next to her ear before he lightly inhaled her scent. There was an almost sensual note in that voice.

She stiffened in his arms, worried about what the hell that meant. Yeah, she might have fantasized about the guy after meeting him once, but that was it.

He let out an angry curse. "I'm not going to hurt you," he growled, as if he'd guessed her train of thought.

"How'd you know I was here?" she demanded even though she had no right to be making any sort of inquiry. Not when she was the intruder, the would-be thief.

"If I let you up, will you run?"

"What do you think?" she snapped, hating that she really liked the feel of him on top of her. She just wished she could turn around and see his face.

"I think you're a fool to break into an alpha's home right in the middle of wolf territory. Your fucking pride sent you? A child?"

Child? An unexpected surge of rage slammed through her. Acting on instinct, she reared back, butting her head right against his face. She didn't hear anything break, but it hurt her head enough that she knew it affected him. Even if he didn't loosen his grip.

He snarled low in his throat. "Damn it, woman. There are shifters outside posted all around the house. I'm letting you up. If you run, I'll tackle you again. And if you manage to get away, another one of my packmates will catch you. They won't be as gentle as me." His voice was low, but it sounded as if he was speaking through clenched teeth.

She knew when to pick her battles and right now she needed to see how much trouble she was in. "Fine. I won't run." At least not yet.

He paused for a moment, then sighed before letting go and moving off her. A very primal part of her actually missed the warmth and weight of his hold. Clearly she had issues. Before she could make a move to push up, he held her under her arms and hauled her up until she was on her feet as if she weighed nothing.

Swallowing hard, she turned to face him. And had to look up.

She'd forgotten how much taller he was than her. Though to be fair, most people were. At five feet, one inch, she hadn't been blessed in the height department.

Captivated by those pale blue eyes, she almost forgot to breathe. Was it possible the giant wolf shifter had actually gotten sexier in six months? She'd convinced herself she'd remembered him wrong. That she'd built up all that raw, masculine sex appeal in her head.

Nope. Her memory wasn't faulty.

A little over a foot taller than her, Max loomed over her, his eyes narrowed, his hard-looking lips pulled into a thin line. She wondered how soft they'd be when he was kissing. Would he be harsh and wild or sweet and gentle? Maybe a mix of both.

"Where's the rest of your pride?" he finally asked, his voice strained.

Blinking, she forced her eyes to meet his, but took a step back. She didn't care if it showed weakness; she needed some distance between them. He started to advance but she held out a hand as she leaned against the edge of the oversized rectangular desk and wrapped her arms around herself. "I'm not going anywhere. And they're not here. It's just me. My sister is getting married in a couple weeks and those jewels should be passed on to her. It's tradition in my pride. Neither my sister nor my mom are part of that *stupid*, ancient feud between Grant's *dead* father and mine. That feud is old and buried and we want back what's rightfully ours."

"Why didn't you set up a meeting with Grant?"

She snorted. "We tried that months ago. Or don't you remember?" Lauren, her parents and two males from her pride had come to talk to Grant about getting the jewels back. They'd been shot down almost immediately. Max had been there to back Grant up. It was stupid, but it stung that their meeting hadn't left an impression on Max. Especially since he'd made quite an impression on her. Even if he had been rude.

"Of course I remember," Max murmured, taking on that low, sensual tone again as his gaze roved over her body with barely concealed appreciation.

She should be annoyed that he was checking her out, but part of her really liked it. Skintight black pants, black boots and a long-sleeved formfitting black T-shirt didn't exactly scream sexy, but she was unintentionally showing off all her curves with the tight fit of her clothes.

He stared at her for a long moment and she could practically see the wheels turning in his head. Though what he was thinking about, she had no clue. "The last time I saw you, you were wearing a strapless green summer dress and gold sandals. And your last words were to tell me to 'fuck off'. I masturbated that night while fantasizing about bending you over the nearest flat surface and fucking you until you were mindless with pleasure."

Lauren blinked, beyond shocked by his crude words. Without thinking she blindly reached for the nearest object on the desk—a paperweight—and chucked it at his head.

With lightning quick reflexes Max caught the moon shaped globe with one hand, then set it on a bookshelf before stalking toward her with the slow, precise movements of a predator.

Out of the corner of her eye she measured the distance to the nearest window. She could jump through the glass and shift mid jump. It would hurt being sliced up by the fragments but she'd heal quickly.

As if he read her mind, he crossed the rest of the distance in the blink of an eye, caging her in with both arms. He placed his hands on the desk on either side of her, but didn't actually touch her.

She swallowed and tried not to let him know how intimidated she was. "How did you know I was here?" she asked quietly, needing to break the silence. She wasn't sure if she should be terrified or turned on and her emotions were all out of whack. His scent made her crazy and the hungry look in his eyes was doing strange things to her insides.

"I scented you on that rock you used to break the French doors. Had a good idea why you did it—good plan by the way. And I knew you'd be back."

"Bullshit. You didn't scent me." But...she didn't scent a lie. It seemed as if he was telling the truth.

His pale eyes narrowed. "Yes. I did. Just like I can scent you now. Like amber and vanilla."

Lauren swallowed hard. There was no way he could be able to scent her. Not with her gift. Unless...she frowned at the thought. No, no, no. That just wasn't possible. She refused to even acknowledge the possibility. Though her gift was rare she knew a few other jaguar shifters with the same ability. The only other shifters able to scent them were their mates.

But there was no way in hell this obnoxious, sexy wolf was her mate.

CHAPTER TWO

Max stared into the big brown eyes of the petite jaguar shifter in front of him. He wanted to kick his own ass for the way he'd just spoken to Lauren. In his pack he was known for being laid back, the one who everyone could come to with their problems if Grant wasn't around. Right now he felt edgy and raw in a way he'd only experienced once before.

The first time he'd met her.

This little minx just brought out something primal in him and he didn't understand it. He did know that he hated the thread of fear in her dark gaze. "I'm not going to hurt you, but you will have to be punished."

Lauren's body tensed, as if she was preparing to fight him. "Punished?"

He leaned closer, still not quite touching her, but he couldn't get enough of her scent. He hadn't been lying when he'd told her he could smell her. It was odd that she was surprised by it. That amber and vanilla scent twined around him like a silk embrace.

She smelled like sex and…his. She smelled like his. It was the only way to describe it. Six months ago when she'd showed up with her parents and pride members he'd been stunned by his raw reaction to her. He'd made a crude comment to her then too—which was why she'd told him to fuck off. She'd seemed so sweet and almost innocent. He'd been angry at himself for noticing her. For wanting her so badly he couldn't see or think straight. Sure twenty-five wasn't young by human standards but he was a hundred and fifty.

He'd fought his feelings for a month then had planned to go after her. But shit had happened that prevented him from chasing after her. He'd had to leave his pack's territory to take care of it and when he'd gotten back he'd been in no condition to court Lauren.

Now she was back in his pack's territory and he wasn't letting her go. His wolf wouldn't let him. In all his years he'd never fought his animal's instinct and he wasn't about to start now. "Yes, punished. You will remain in Kincaid territory for a week. You will stay with me, under my roof. At the end of the week—seven full days starting *tomorrow*—you can go home. With your brooch." *Liar*, his inner wolf howled. Max didn't want to let her go home.

But he knew Grant would give her pride the jewels back. They'd talked about it last month. After some issues with rogue vampires a few months ago Grant had decided it wouldn't hurt to be cordial to any packs or prides in the nearby area. Shifters had long lives and long memories and having a pride pissed at his pack for something that happened a century ago wasn't smart. His alpha just hadn't gotten around to contacting the Hayes pride because he'd been too wrapped up in his new mate.

Lauren shoved at his chest with surprising strength, the flash of anger and...hurt in her gaze cutting into him. "I'm not a whore."

His eyebrows raised and he didn't move from his spot, though he could feel the imprint of where she'd struck him. "I didn't say you'd have to sleep with me. Just that you're *staying* with me." Though he did want her in his bed. In his shower, on the floor, anywhere she'd let him take her.

Confusion rolled off her in palpable waves, the tension in her compact, delicious body loosening. "You just want me to stay with you?"

He nodded and she seemed even more confused.

"Why?" Her gaze darkened as she seemed to have another thought. "I'm not going to be your freaking maid either."

Max shrugged and struggled to verbalize his thoughts in a way that wouldn't sound insane. "My punishment, my reason. And no, you won't be required to do anything other than shadow me. With Grant gone I'm in charge. Take the deal or I'll let my pack deal with you." He wouldn't—no way in hell would he let anyone touch her. Not that the Kincaid pack would actually do anything to her. Yeah, they were wolves, but they preferred to live and let live. Senseless violence was not tolerated and anyone with that mentality was kicked out or killed if deemed too much of a threat. Their pack had carved out a nice territory and for at least the next decade they planned to live here in peace.

"You're not going to try to hurt me?" There was an underlying edge of steel in her voice and he didn't miss the word 'try'. Because a woman like her wouldn't let anyone get the best of her. Not without shredding them to ribbons.

Angered that she would think that, Max shoved away from the desk, putting a few feet between them. Not that it did anything to lessen his electric pull to her. "Is your pride in the habit of hurting females?"

Now she looked shocked. "No!"

"Then why would you assume I would hurt you? We respect females regardless of species. Your punishment is simple. Stay under my roof for seven days, you get the jewels. And if you don't...I won't give you to my pack. They'd never hurt you either. I shouldn't have insinuated that. But you'll be sent home and won't get your family heirloom." The truth was in his voice and his scent.

She gritted her teeth. "You swear I'll get the brooch? Your alpha will have no problem with this?"

Max nodded. "I swear it."

She looked conflicted about whether she believed him, but nodded. "Fine. One week. I need to call my pride members and let them know."

Max pulled his phone out of his pocket and handed it to her. "Go ahead. Do it now." The sooner he could get her back to his place, the better. He wanted her scent invading his home, his sheets, his bed. Of course that was going to take some persuasion. He looked forward to it.

Lauren looked surprised, but shook her head. Bending down, she retrieved a slim cell from her boot. "I've got one."

With her skintight outfit it had been hard to tell where she could have possibly hidden one. Turning her back to him, she made a call and hurriedly explained the situation. Max could hear a male on the other end and fought an irrational jealousy swelling inside him. The male argued with her, but Lauren was firm that the pride let her do this and not to interfere. As she spoke, he couldn't stop his gaze from wandering over the length of her body.

Though she was petite, her body was taut and lean in the way most jaguars were. But he couldn't see her hair thanks to that ridiculous knitted cap. When Max had scented her on that rock it was like his wolf had come alive again. Ever since that meeting with her pride he'd been edgy and moody, lashing out at random pack members.

To have her under the same roof as him was too much. While she talked, he reached out and snagged the cap off her head.

Startled, she glanced over her shoulder, but he just shrugged and tucked her cap into his back pocket. Her thick, honey brown hair fell past her shoulders in soft waves. She raked her fingers through the long tresses and turned away from him, continuing her conversation. Whoever was on the other end was annoyed, but she wasn't taking no for an answer.

As she finger combed her hair, all he could fantasize about was what it would be like to run his own fingers through it while she was naked and on top of him, or bent over his bed or—

Lauren turned to face him, her phone call over. "It's a done deal. I don't have any of my clothes though."

"What hotel were you at?"

Her lips pursed into a thin line and he realized that if she told him, he'd know where the rest of her pridemates were staying too. It would only take a few phone calls to find out anyway. He decided not to point that out.

Max scrubbed a hand over his face. He wouldn't hurt them, but he didn't want to get into an argument with her. "One of your pridemates can drop your bags off at my place. I give you my word they won't be hurt or harassed. But they have to leave our territory afterward." He rattled off the address then let her make the decision about what she wanted to do. Either she believed him or she didn't.

Using the phone still in her hand, she texted someone with a ridiculous speed. After a few back and forth texts, she tucked the phone into her boot again.

"I've never seen anyone type that fast." Her fingers had flown across the keyboard like lightning.

She shrugged. "Your generation doesn't seem to embrace technology like mine." There was a bite of sarcasm in her words as she insinuated he was old, and he realized it was because he'd called her a child.

Something she definitely wasn't. She was very grown and very sensual. He just grunted and motioned with his head that she should follow him. He'd already disabled the alarm and as soon as he and Lauren stepped outside, another of his packmates would be babysitting the house. Where they lived they'd never had a problem with crime of either the human or supernatural variety but until Grant got back, Max was keeping his alpha's house under constant watch. He didn't trust Lauren's pridemates not to do something stupid.

He trusted her—though he wasn't sure why—but he didn't know her pride and it was his duty to keep the pack's territory under control while Grant was on his honeymoon.

As they stepped outside, Max could see two of his packmates standing at attention in the lush front yard. The back was a smaller yard, a pool and the rest of the property stretched all the way to the beach where more of his packmates waited. He'd been relatively positive that Lauren would come back but he hadn't been sure if there would be more of her pridemates with her or what their intention had been—though he'd guessed it would be about the jewels.

Even if he'd been glad to find her in his alpha's office, it enraged him that her pride had sent her into enemy territory alone. All over some fucking jewels. Sure they were worth a few million, but she was worth more than that. If she were his, he'd never have let her do something so dangerous.

He couldn't see the rest of his packmates, but he could scent a dozen of them nearby. So could Lauren. And he could smell her fear even though it was clear she was trying to mask it. On instinct, he wrapped an arm around her shoulders as they stepped off the porch and down the few stone steps.

She tensed but didn't pull away—something that soothed his inner wolf immensely.

"Lauren Hayes is under my protection and staying with me," he said, slightly raising his voice though everyone seen and unseen would be able to hear him. "Her pridemates are also under my protection. One of them will be coming by the condo later so let them leave Lauren's belongings at the front gate with no hassle." He didn't go into any more detail because he didn't have to.

As second-in-command, his pack would respect what he'd said. And they'd also spread the word, letting the entire pack know she would be in Kincaid territory with him. Which was good and bad. Shifters were the biggest gossips around. He knew he'd be fielding calls and drop-ins all day tomorrow with packmates wanting to get a look at the jaguar shifter who'd broken into Grant's house. They'd want to know why the hell Max was protecting her and why she was under his roof.

He didn't owe them those answers. Lauren was his and he wasn't letting her go.

CHAPTER THREE

Max opened the door to his condo then bolted it shut. Normally he left his door unlocked during the day, as did most of the pack, but after the last few hours of putting out bullshit fires for his packmates, he didn't want to see anyone else.

Except Lauren.

She'd been sleeping when he'd left early this morning to deal with the accountant at the hotel the pack owned. He'd left a note and his cell number to call if she needed anything but she hadn't.

Something he found disappointing. He'd been thinking about her all damn day, much to his annoyance. She'd been quiet when they got back to his place last night. Not rude or temperamental like he'd expected, but almost withdrawn instead. He guessed she was still trying to figure out what the hell he was up to by 'punishing' her with staying with him. Part of him had been tempted to wake her and take her with him today but he'd had too much to deal with and he could admit he was selfish. He wanted to get to know her when it was just the two of them and in better circumstances than him working.

Part of him had feared she'd split the second she woke up, but he'd been banking on the fact that she wanted that brooch too much. He'd heard through the grapevine of pack gossip that she was still here and had been taking pack visitors all day with incredible politeness.

Her scent and something that smelled incredible teased him as he headed down the hallway in the direction of the kitchen. She'd cooked? Each packmate had an ocean view and since he had the penthouse of the condominium building the pack owned, his place was a little larger than most.

The hallway emptied out into an open living room and kitchen, with the kitchen to the left. As he stepped into the normally unused room, he froze in his tracks. Bent over pulling something out of the oven, Lauren wore skimpy little shorts that rode up and almost showed the bottom of her ass. Swallowing hard, Max forced himself to look away as he stepped into the kitchen. She had to know he was there. She'd have heard the door opening and scented him. Maybe she was waiting for him to speak first.

He'd acted like an asshole last night when he'd told her his fantasies about her and he needed to get himself under control. Staring at her ass wouldn't help him.

Clearing his throat as he stepped into the room, he tossed his keys onto the counter and headed for the refrigerator. "Something smells good," he said in what he hoped was a casual voice as he grabbed a beer.

"I got bored so I decided to cook. Hope you like shepherd's pie." Her sweet voice wrapped around him, making him light headed for a moment. God, how could she have this affect on him?

Shutting the fridge, he found her slipping the oven mitts off and turning to face him. She smiled tentatively. "Listen, I know we got off on the wrong foot and that your punishment, even though it's a little odd, isn't harsh. If I'm gonna be here for a week, I'd like to be at least civil." There was a question in her eyes even though she didn't ask anything. Her cooking dinner was a sort of peace offering.

One he would gladly take. He nodded, forcing his gaze not to trail down her lean, lithe body. Despite the cooler weather she wore barely there yoga shorts and a tank top. With their higher body temperatures it made sense, plus he'd left the heat on. Her hair was pulled up into a messy ponytail with tendrils framing her face and with no makeup she looked so comfortable, like she belonged here. In his home. "That works for me. You want a drink?"

She nodded so he grabbed another beer. When he shut the fridge again he watched her moving around his kitchen with ease. She set plates and utensils out on the island before moving the glass baking dish to the cooling rack she'd set out. He hadn't even realized he owned a cooling rack. He rarely used the room, choosing to eat at one of the restaurants the pack owned. She seemed so at home and she'd clearly figured out where everything was.

Feeling almost useless and not wanting to get in her way, he sat at the island and set both their beers down. "How'd you manage to cook all this?" He knew he didn't have the ingredients to make shepherd's pie. Or anything at all except maybe an omelet.

"Some of your packmates stopped by so I hit them up for ingredients. I didn't know if I was allowed to leave your place," she said with a slight smile but he knew she wasn't kidding.

Punishments for invading another supernatural's territory could be harsh or nothing at all. It just depended on the crime and the alpha involved. Since she'd actually broken into an alpha's home, Max could have done a lot worse. Something she knew and was another reason he hadn't worried about her leaving. She'd gotten off incredibly easy with his punishment. "You could have called and asked."

She shrugged and sat next to him. "I didn't want to bug you, especially since I had company from pretty much the moment I woke up. Your pack is very nosy."

Their chairs were a foot apart, but he could feel her body heat and desperately wanted to slide closer, to inhale her sweet scent. Instead of doing what he wanted, he added a helping to her plate, then his. "Is your pride any different?"

She snorted and let out a short laugh. "No way. They're horrible. When I go home I already know what kind of gossip will have been spread. I'm pretty sure your packmates think we're getting mated or something. Some of those older women are ready to see you settled and call me crazy, I don't think they care if it's with a jaguar." She laughed again, as if the idea was ridiculous. "They got so excited when I told them I wanted to cook you dinner." Shaking her head, she took a bite of her meal.

He watched her swallow and tried to ignore the way she'd laughed about the idea of them mating. Yeah, it was uncommon but not unheard of. It bothered him that she thought it was funny, even though he knew he shouldn't have this reaction.

"Do you not like it?" Lauren asked and he realized he was staring at her.

Clearing his throat, he turned his attention back to his plate and took a bite of his meal. It was good. *Really* good. Of course it could have tasted like sandpaper and he would have told her it was the best meal he'd ever had. "This is great, thanks for cooking. I don't expect you to though."

"I wanted to." She shrugged again as if it was no big deal and he struggled to read her. He could scent her natural amber and vanilla as strong as anything, but normally he could read more than that with others. He hated that he couldn't tell much about her emotions. His wolf senses were how he read people.

"Listen, I've got to head to The Crescent Moon Bar tonight for a couple hours." Max normally managed there, but with Grant gone Max had divided his time between all the places the pack owned and tonight was when he visited his normal bar. He wanted Lauren with him when he went. "Come with me?"

She set her fork back down on her plate. "Do I have a choice?"

There was no sarcasm in her question. He realized she was being serious. He could order her if he wanted. His most primal side wanted to. He'd felt edgy all damn day without her—something he was still trying to understand. "Yes."

She smiled then, a real one, the effect stunning as it relaxed her entire face. "Okay. I've been cooped up here all day so it'll be nice to get out. Your pack has been really great." She sounded surprised by that.

Relief settled through him that she wanted to go, even if it was just to get out. Tonight he had to show her that he wasn't the asshole who'd said he wanted to bend her over the nearest flat surface and fuck her. He cringed at himself, even if what he'd said was true. Inwardly sighing, he took another bite. He just hoped he could keep his primal side in check tonight.

* * *

As they stepped into the Crescent Moon Bar, Lauren was consciously aware of Max's large hand on the small of her back. It should have been a casual move, but she felt as if he was branding her in some way. The heat generating from him was unmistakable but she was doing her best to cover the scent of her attraction and her expressions. So far she was pretty sure it was working. He seemed to be able to smell her natural scent but nothing beyond that. Of course she was concentrating really hard on masking her attraction to him. She didn't want him using it against her and she really didn't want to do something she'd regret. But if he kept touching her, she didn't know how long she could keep it up.

In addition to her gift to cover her scent, as the youngest of the Hayes sisters, she'd learned how to school her expressions at an early age thanks to her older sisters. With her father being the alpha, she'd needed to keep a few things from him if she'd ever wanted to have any fun as a teenager.

Which was why her father didn't actually know she was here in Gulf Shores. He thought she was on vacation.

Man, he was going to be so pissed when he found out. Two of her sisters knew that she and a handful of her cousins had decided to come after the brooch so they could give it as a gift to her oldest sister, Stacia. They wouldn't say anything to her father though.

Lauren inwardly sighed. Stacia would be angry at that risk they'd taken but it was going to work out now and no one was getting hurt. Grant had a reputation for being honest and if Max said she'd get the jewels, she would. If at the end of the week he lied, however, then there would be an all-out war between her pride and the Kincaid pack. She knew no one wanted that.

Well, no one in their right mind. Shifters didn't like to attract attention to themselves so while yes, she was taking a risk by staying here a week and walking away with nothing, something bone deep told her that Max wasn't lying.

Two steps inside the bar, Lauren realized the place was in chaos. There was no other word for it. In college she'd waited tables—something that had driven her parents crazy since they hadn't wanted her to work—and from what she could see there were only two women on the floor and one woman behind the bar. Clearly they were overwhelmed.

"Shit," Max muttered next to her. Then taking her by surprise, he grabbed her hand and headed for a swinging door she knew would lead to a kitchen.

Inside was one woman lifting up a large oval tray filled with plates of hamburgers and other grill style meals. She gave Max a frazzled look and didn't even bother glancing at Lauren. "We need help at the bar!" she growled before hurrying toward the swinging doors.

Two males were behind the grill line and one of them jerked a thumb behind him. "In the office."

Lauren didn't know what that meant, but Max just growled under his breath. Seconds later she stood with him in the entryway to a small office that had a computer, a small desk, and stacks of papers. Jeez, they were unorganized. A tall woman with blond hair was on the phone shouting at someone 'to get their asses over here' but she slammed the phone down when she saw Max. "Almost everyone is out with some bullshit excuse. It's fucking madness and I can't get anyone to come in here because they're already working at one of the other restaurants or the hotel. I've been helping man the grill line but we need someone helping behind the bar and someone taking the drinks for the servers. If it wasn't for the alcoholic drinks the girls would be fine but they keep having—"

"I can serve the drinks," Lauren said quickly, interrupting the woman's frantic machine-gun fire of words. There was no reason *not* to help. Not when the Kincaid pack had been so nice to her—after she'd broken into their alpha's home. Yeah, she needed to show some goodwill to this pack and had no problem pitching in.

Max turned to look at her then, his expression stunned.

"What?" she demanded, unnerved by his intense stare.

"Why are you offering?" His suspicious tone pissed her off.

Lauren reined in her temper. She shrugged, not wanting to admit that 1) she simply wanted to help his pack out because she felt freaking guilty and 2) it would put some distance between the two of them. "It's not like I have anything better to do to. But if you don't want the help, fine," she gritted out.

His gaze swept over her attire then landed back at her face. She could tell he didn't want her to, but she wasn't sure why. The women she'd seen working had on black pants, black tops and black aprons. Right now Lauren wore a corset-style lace up black top and jeans. With an apron covering her jeans, she'd fit in well enough. Before he could open his mouth to argue or make another rude comment, the woman behind him smacked his arm.

"Do you have any experience in restaurants?" she asked, the tension rolling off her almost palpable.

Reaching in her back pocket to grab a hair band, Lauren said, "I waited tables in college. Just let me see a layout of the restaurant so I know how each table section is labeled. I'll start with delivering all the bar drinks and if you need me to deliver food to tables once they get that under control, I will." She swept her hair up into a ponytail so it would be out of her face.

The blond woman grabbed Max's arm and yanked him so he had to look back at her. "What are you waiting for? We're drowning out there!"

Cringing, Lauren wondered if the woman's only volume setting was loud.

Max let out a curse and gave Lauren another suspicious look. "Fine. I'll help at the bar and she can serve the drinks. But see if you can get her a T-shirt or something."

"My top is fine," Lauren snapped. What the hell was wrong with him? She was a jaguar and wasn't going to put on someone else's top. Their scent would be all over her and drive her insane.

The blonde ignored Max and practically shoved past the giant wolf and dragged Lauren away. After introducing herself as Sapphire—yes, freaking Sapphire—she shoved an apron at Lauren then dragged her to the bar to introduce her to the bartender, a female named Charlie.

The bartender had long, brown hair and was moving around with the speed of only a supernatural but it was clear she was still behind on her orders. The thick pile of tickets next to the cash register was proof enough. After tying her apron on, Lauren quickly scanned the laminated layout Sapphire practically threw at her before she'd darted away.

Lauren looked at the layout of the restaurant and bar area, then back at the printout one more time. She had a knack for being able to look at something once or twice and remember most of the details. "Leave the ticket with the drinks and I'll figure out where they're going." There was no way she'd have time to learn the computer system so waiting tables and taking orders was out of the question. But this she could easily do. And it soothed her conscience to help out Max this way. Even if the brooch belonged to her family she still felt guilty after seeing how nice this pack truly was.

Charlie nodded at her, her expression grateful. "Thanks," she said before turning back to where she was three-deep at the bar.

Damn, the woman really needed help. Lauren poked her head back into the kitchen, ready to tell Max to hurry up and help the woman out when she stopped dead in her tracks.

A tall, lithe woman with black hair and wearing a skimpy black dress—clearly not waitstaff—was plastered up against Max, her arms wrapped around him and her lips crushing his.

It was like Lauren had been punched in the stomach. All the air rushed out of her lungs and the noisy surroundings faded to nothing as a buzz filled her ears. Something dark inside her flared to life, her inner jaguar wanting to claw the unknown woman to shreds. And Max for that matter. The reaction was ridiculous but so primal, so visceral it took her by surprise.

Though it felt like an eternity, only seconds had passed before Max stepped back. In that instant he found her watching him, his expression one of surprise and another emotion she couldn't define. Lauren didn't care what it was. She schooled her expression. "If you can tear yourself away, your help is needed at the bar," she said coldly before turning on her heel and letting the door swing closed behind her.

Unsure what was wrong with her, why she felt almost betrayed, Lauren picked up a large tray next to the end of the bar and started loading three separate orders on them. She picked table numbers that were clustered together so she could make the least trips possible and get things out as fast as she could. As she started to lift the tray, Max came up beside her and lifted the hatch to the bar.

"Lauren, that woman isn't—"

"What you do is none of my business." She wasn't sure what he'd been about to say, but all she knew was, she didn't want to hear it. She didn't want to hear anything out of his stupid mouth right now.

CHAPTER FOUR

"Damn, Max, give the girl a break," Charlie muttered next him as she loaded another glass into a bin, getting it ready to take to one of the dishwashers in the back.

"What the hell are you talking about?" he growled, unable to hide his annoyance as he wiped down one of the liquor bottles. It was close to two in the morning and most of the restaurant was cleared out except a few tables. The actual bar was already closed and while he wanted nothing more than to throw Lauren over his shoulder and get the hell out of there, he wouldn't leave his packmate Charlie alone to clean up the bar. Not when Sapphire and the other servers were already busting ass to clean the back of the house and tables.

Lauren had offered to help, but Sapphire had told her not to worry about it because of all her help tonight. Yeah, she'd been helpful but she'd also flirted with every single guy she'd waited on. Maybe that was a bit of a stretch but it sure felt like it. So now she was sitting at a table with some of his male packmates laughing and looking too gorgeous for her own good. And for his sanity.

Her hair was still pulled up into a ponytail, revealing her long neck and with how low her top was cut, she was baring too much skin. Shoulders shouldn't be sexy, but hers were. He wanted to rake his teeth over all her exposed skin then follow up with kisses. He wanted to mark her so all other males would know she was off limits.

"You're staring at her as if she's the enemy. What she did was fucked up but...Grant should have given those damn jewels back to her pride. We all know it and it's not like our pack needs the money." Before Max could interrupt Charlie continued. "Besides, she gave us all her tips from tonight to split. She's okay in my book. By the way, whatever happened to that skank human you hook up with sometimes?" Charlie asked in disgust, not bothering to hide her annoyance. "Thought I saw her in here earlier."

Max sighed and rubbed a hand over his face. "She's not a...don't talk about her like that. And we're through." They had been for over six months. Or so he'd assumed. Things between him and Darcie had fizzled over six months ago and she stopped coming around right before he'd met Lauren for the first time. After getting her scent into his system neither he nor his wolf wanted anyone else so it had worked out perfect for him that the human female was out of the picture. It wasn't like they'd ever been a couple and that had worked fine for both of them. It only made sense things had ended between them with no drama.

Then she'd showed up tonight drunk, angry at her new boyfriend for some reason, so she'd thrown herself at Max. Of course Lauren had seen her kissing him. She'd been hard to read but for a fraction of a second, she'd looked raging pissed at him. His primal side had been glad she actually cared, but he hadn't wanted to hurt her even inadvertently.

"Good," Charlie muttered. "Why don't you get out of here? I know you've been dealing with all of Grant's duties and we've got this covered. Get some rest."

Under normal circumstances he would have argued, but one of his packmates, Derrick, had just handed Lauren a folded up piece of paper. Likely with his number on it. Max's inner wolf went crazy when she tucked it into the front of her jeans pocket and smiled at the other wolf. "Thanks, see ya later," he muttered before ducking out from behind the bar.

He covered the distance between the bar and the table to Lauren in seconds. Derrick glanced up at him, an easy smile on his face. "Hey, man, we're—"

Max ignored him, keeping his focus on Lauren. "We're leaving."

She blinked, probably surprised by his harsh tone.

He hadn't meant to demand it, but his inner wolf needed her away from these other males. The most primal part of him was feeling edgy and possessive. His canines ached, begging to be released. He wanted to flash them at his packmates as a warning to back the fuck off but he kept himself in check. Barely.

"Come on man, hang out for a little longer." Derrick, one of the part-time bouncers at the bar, was a good guy. Hell, one of the most decent packmates Max had, but right now, he didn't give a shit.

He knew his wolf was in his eyes because Lauren just stood, pushing her chair back and moving to his side with a fluid grace that turned him on even as he was annoyed with her. Her nearness soothed him somewhat, but not nearly enough. Moving lightning fast, he reached into the front of her pocket and pulled out the paper Derrick had given her.

He let his claws extend, shredding the paper into confetti. She gasped and the entire table—and the waitstaff—went silent. The pieces silently fell to the floor. "She's not going to be calling you." Even though he spoke to Derrick, he kept his gaze on her.

Fire erupted in Lauren's eyes, her inner jaguar peeking through as they transformed into straight feline, amber and glowing with anger. "I'll call whoever I want."

"You want to do this right here?" he asked, his voice silky smooth.

For a long moment she didn't answer, as if she was weighing her options. Then without glancing at the table or anyone else in the bar, she strode for the exit, her head held high and that perfect ass of hers swaying in such an erotic rhythm that he wasn't able to contain the growl he let out.

"Listen Max, I'm sorry, I didn't realize you two—" Derrick started, but Max cut him off.

"It's fine. But she's taken." There was no other explanation needed and right now he was going after her. Whether she wanted to hear him out or not, he was going to explain what had happened with Darcie.

Lauren had been cold to him all night and he knew it was because of the human female. So even if he couldn't scent Lauren's attraction, he knew she felt something.

And he planned to take full advantage of that.

Once outside, he frowned when Lauren wasn't waiting like he'd expected. Following her scent trail that still didn't give him a hint of her emotions, he headed east down a quiet street that lead straight to the beach. Crescent Moon Bar wasn't directly on the beach but it was close. His annoyance grew as he jogged over the only cross-street and continued until he ran into a deck that led to the sandy shore and calm ocean. As he reached the end of it, he saw Lauren's clothes in a neat pile. Including a very skimpy black thong. Sexual hunger slammed into him, as if he'd been physically tackled. The thought of her wearing it—or nothing at all—consumed him.

She'd likely assumed it was late enough that she wouldn't run into any humans when she shifted to her jaguar form and could come back for her clothes later. On the off chance there were humans out now, Lauren would be able to blend in using the shadows.

That knowledge still didn't soothe him any. Picking up her clothes, he followed her scent trail down the beach all the way to his condo. The anger grew inside him with each step he'd taken that she'd left like that. Without a word. He didn't want to admit it, but he'd feared she'd actually left for good.

He knew he didn't have any claim on her, but she was still under his jurisdiction. The thought was bitter though. He didn't want her here because she was serving a sentence he meted out. He wanted her here because she wanted to be with him.

That knowledge scared the shit out of him. He'd been trying to deny it but all day he'd been hungry, almost crazed to get back to her. Deep down he knew what it meant even if he couldn't bring himself to admit it. If he made himself vulnerable to her and he was wrong—Max shut that thought down before it finished.

Shoving those thoughts aside, he reined his wolf in as he shut and locked the door behind him. Trailing after her amber and vanilla scent wasn't necessary since he could hear the shower running in one of the guest bathrooms. He told himself to stop, to wait until she was out, but his need to see her overrode his rational brain. He wanted her to acknowledge the desire between them. And like a randy cub, he wanted her to stop ignoring him.

The door to her bedroom was shut, but he opened it and headed straight for the one that led to the bathroom, which was cracked open. Wisps of steam billowed out from the opening. Using all his stealth and quickness—before he could change his mind—he fully opened the door, crossed the tile floor in a few quick strides and dragged the shower curtain back with a loud jangle.

Standing under the powerful showerhead, Lauren's eyes snapped open in shock. She stood there frozen before her hands went to cover her naked breasts. But not before he saw the light brown color of her tightly beaded nipples. Instantly his cock hardened to the point it was almost painful. He wanted to drag her hands away, to look his fill of her luscious body.

In a delayed realization, it hit him that she'd had one of her hands between her legs. Had she been stroking herself? The thought of that was insanely hot. Before he could dwell on that mental image, she blindly grabbed for a washcloth and slapped it at him, hitting his shoulder with a wet snap. She dropped it when she realized she'd left one of her breasts exposed to hit him.

"What the hell are you doing?" Her voice was a screech of panic. "Get out of here now!"

He crossed his arms over his chest as he struggled to keep his eyes on her face instead of roving over her body like he craved. He shouldn't have come in here like this but he didn't care. He needed her to *see* him, to acknowledge the heat burning between them. Needed her to want him as much as he wanted her. "Why the fuck did you leave like that?"

"I'm not having this conversation while I'm naked." Her eyes narrowed on him in warning. And damn it, he still couldn't scent any desire coming from her even though he knew damn well she'd had her hand buried between her legs a minute ago. Had she been thinking of him while she stroked herself? His cock swelled even more.

"Would it make you feel better if I was naked too?" he murmured, ready to strip completely. His blood pounded hot and heavy through his veins, pulsed in his cock. The wolf was there, clawing for freedom and the chance to take what it wanted. Lauren. Wet and naked and willing, responding to his every touch, each nip of his mouth on her smooth skin.

"No," she snapped before grabbing the shower curtain to cover herself. She held it up above her breasts, the water splashing over it and spraying everywhere. "Have you lost your mind?"

Max certainly felt like it. He'd never reacted to a female this way. Before he could respond, she continued.

"You don't get to tell me who I can or can't talk to. I'll take phone numbers from every guy in that bar next time I'm there. We made our deal and that was that I was to stay with you, which *I've done*. I even helped out at your pack's bar. What I didn't agree to, was letting you push me around or harass me while I'm naked in the shower."

He was silent for a moment as he watched her breathing become erratic. The rise and fall of her chest was unsteady and the anger rolling off her was palpable, but he also scented something else. Desire. Triumph rolled through him. His inner wolf growled in pleasure. Everything she'd said was true. He shouldn't have come in here, but there was no reining his wolf in right now. Max didn't want walls between them.

"Were you touching yourself when I walked in here?"

She hissed in a breath, but didn't respond. Just swallowed hard and glared at him. Holy shit, she had been.

"What were you thinking of? Me?" Yeah, it was arrogant to ask. But he needed to know.

She rolled her eyes, but he didn't miss the way she subtly trembled. "You wish."

He did. Knowing he needed to clear the air, he said, "That woman from earlier kissed me, not the other way around. We've been done for a long time. She came in tonight and was drunk. You saw me pushing her off. Nothing more. And I'm not sleeping with anyone right now. Haven't been for over six months." Let her make of that what she wanted.

Lauren's hand slackened slightly, the shower curtain dipping low enough to show the soft swell of her breasts, but still covering her. "Why do you think I care?"

He saw the indecision warring in her eyes, and pounced on it. "You care for the same reason I wanted to claw Derrick to shreds for giving you his number. For the same reason I wanted to do the same to every male you flirted with tonight. You're mine." Admitting that made him feel vulnerable, but he knew he had to put himself out there.

Her lips parted a fraction, surprise in her gaze. She watched him, her eyes wide and that same scent of desire still rolling off her. It was growing stronger each second that passed, but she still didn't say anything or reach for him.

Finally he forced himself to take a step back, ready to leave. There was nothing else to say. And if he stayed, his wolf would win the fight and he'd be naked and taking her against the shower wall in seconds.

"Don't go," she said, so softly he barely heard her words above the rushing water. He stopped, unsure if it was the invitation he'd been dying for. Then she dropped the shower curtain, baring all of herself to him. No hands covering herself this time, though she looked incredibly nervous.

He barely stifled a growl at the sight of her naked body. Petite, lean and soft in all the right places, she was his hottest fantasy come to life. With her honey brown hair wet it appeared darker as it fell in ropes over and around her breasts.

His throat clenched as he struggled to talk. "I want you." Fucking understatement of the century.

She tracked his every move with those big brown eyes. When he stripped his shirt off, her eyes grew heavy as she watched him. It was almost as if she was mesmerized by what he was doing. He took off his jeans, but kept his boxers on. It was a struggle in control, forcing him to go against all of his instincts, but it was *necessary*.

Frowning, she opened her mouth to say something as he stepped into the shower, but he placed one finger over her lips as he grabbed her bare hip and tugged her close with his other hand. "If these come off, I'll be inside you, fucking hard and rough. Right now I don't want that." Okay, that was a huge lie. He wanted exactly that. But…he wanted to taste her, to learn her body first. She deserved it and even though his wolf was raging at him, clawing and snarling with a vengeance to take what he wanted, he knew on a primal level that if he pushed her too far, too fast tonight it could damage his chance with her.

Though she kept her smoldering gaze on his, her swallow was audible as she reached up to place her delicate hands on his shoulders. Her touch seared him. The second her fingers made contact, his hands fisted on her hips and he lifted her up, moving until he had her flat against the wall.

She wrapped her legs around him, her bare pussy rubbing against his lower abdomen. Max let out a soft growl. He kept her up high enough on his body that she wasn't directly rubbing over his cock. Not yet. He wasn't that much of a masochist.

Lauren molded her lean body to his as she linked her fingers together at the back of his neck. He loved that she still held his gaze, even when he could see the nervousness lurking there. "Do you feel…" She trailed off, almost as if she wasn't sure how to continue, but he knew what she meant.

"The fucking strongest attraction I've ever experienced in my entire life?" Attraction was such a lame word for what he felt. Magnetic pull, hunger, desire…even those didn't describe his need.

She nodded and pushed out a breath, her hard nipples rubbing against his chest. "I'm glad I'm not the only one. I've been trying to…hide my need for you but it's killing me."

It was the same for him. Holding her so close, feeling her lush, naked body against was soothing the most primal part of him, even as it was making him insane with desire.

Lauren was his and he wanted her to know it in every cell of her being. Before he was through with her tonight, she would. Reaching between their bodies, he cupped one of her breasts, holding it firmly as he began to slowly stroke her nipple. Their embrace was intimate and he was going into sensory overload having Lauren naked and in his arms, but they had all the time in the world and he refused to rush this. He wanted to see her reaction to every single touch.

"Did you flirt with those shifters tonight to make me jealous?" he growled.

"Yes." Her answer was immediate and non-apologetic.

He lightly pinched her nipple and she gasped. She arched her back, pushing her breast farther into his hold, another pleasured sound escaping her lips.

Unable to stop himself, he cupped the back of her head in a dominating grip and covered her mouth with his. Her lips were soft, pliable and she opened immediately for him. Her tongue stroked against his, her kisses teasing and playful as she wrapped her legs tighter around his waist.

Continuing to strum her nipple in lazy movements, he blazed a trail of kisses away from her mouth, down her jaw line and to her ear, only stopping to rake his teeth over the spot below her ear. She shivered in his arms. "I didn't like it. Never again, Lauren. You're mine." A delayed admission to her answer.

"Well I didn't like that woman kissing you," she rasped out, another moan escaping when he lightly tugged on her earlobe with his teeth.

Max could only imagine how he'd react if another male had kissed her. But even the thought of that made his inner wolf swipe out in anger so he shoved it away.

Lauren was on fire, burning up from the inside out. She reached between their bodies, running her hand down his washboard abs in a slow, determined path. She wanted to feel his hard length between her hands. But when she reached the top of his boxers, the strong hand cupping her head moved with supernatural speed to stop her.

Max lightly grasped her wrist, his fingers slightly flexing. "No."

The word sounded almost guttural, torn from him with clear effort. His wolf flashed in his gaze for a second before once again she was looking into pale blue eyes that made her lose all her common sense. Her entire body was primed for this male, ready to take him deep inside her. She was already soaked. Had been from the moment he'd displayed all that dominance and shredded the phone number that shifter had given her. It had angered her, but mainly turned her on.

Then when Max had barged into her bathroom a tiny part of her had been outraged, but she'd been glad he followed her from the bar. It was all part of her animal instinct, she knew that. But she'd never cared for the male-female chase before.

Tonight she'd finally understood why her oldest sister had led her soon-to-be mate around on a merry chase for months.

There was a thrill in being pursued and she wanted to enjoy a week of raw sex with Max. Talk about the best punishment ever. She knew there was no viable way for them to be together long term—not when he was a wolf and she was a jaguar—but for now she could enjoy herself. And lord, she'd never wanted a man as badly as she wanted him. She wanted to feel all that raw power unleashed on her, to be the focus of his formidable sexual energy, even just once.

She didn't understand why he wouldn't let her touch him though. She wanted to wrap her fingers around his cock and feel him slide deep into her. "Why?" she tried to demand, though the question came our breathless and unsteady.

In response he kissed her, his crushing lips hard and dominating. His tongue invaded her mouth as he rolled his hips against her. She gasped at the feel of his thick erection pressed against her. His kisses mimicked sex—no, fucking. There was something primal about the way he was stroking his tongue against hers. Flicking, teasing and hungry, he didn't let up on his assault and she didn't want him to.

She slid down his body until his covered erection rubbed over her wet slit, coming in contact with her pulsing clit. While she hadn't seen that part of him yet, what she could feel was impressive.

She was aching for him, her body on fire with the kind of need only he could sate. She'd had only a couple lovers in the past and they'd always left her wanting. Right now she was more turned on by Max than she'd ever been and it was because of the power he radiated, because of the way he looked at her, made her feel. Like she was the most beautiful woman on the planet.

Taking her off guard, he tore his mouth from hers, his breathing uneven, his eyes flashing from wolf to human. As if he was barely holding onto his control. The tense muscles beneath her hands quivered with restraint.

Before she realized his intent, he gripped her hips and dropped to his knees. But there was nothing submissive about his gesture.

"Put one leg over my shoulder," he commanded.

A demand she would gladly follow. Hot water flowed from the showerhead, spraying both of them as she lifted her right leg and placed her foot on his shoulder. In this position she felt so exposed and almost vulnerable but he didn't give her time to think.

His mouth zeroed in on her most sensitive area, his tongue licking along the length of her wet slit, up and down, over and over before he pushed his tongue inside her, tasting, teasing.

Dropping her head back against the tile wall, she closed her eyes and let herself just feel. She threaded her fingers through his dark hair as he pleasured her, her inner walls clenching to be filled completely. As if he read her mind, Max slid his fingers inside her. He didn't test her slickness with one, he just pushed two right into her.

Thrusting deep, he curled his fingers against the sensitive spot that drove her insane and began stroking her as he worked her clit with his tongue. The sensations were too much, pushing her over the edge before she was prepared.

Nipples tingling in the most delicious way, she arched her back off the wall as the beginning of her climax rippled through her. It built and built, the sensation pushing out to all her nerve endings as Max continued teasing her body, until suddenly she felt as if she was in a freefall.

The orgasm slammed into her, pleasure overtaking everything as she gripped his head, holding onto him so she wouldn't collapse. She tried to bite back her shouts, but couldn't restrain her cries. The moans fell freely from her lips as the pleasure rocked through her. She wasn't sure how long it lasted, but it seemed to go on forever until her knees weakened. Feeling almost boneless, she could barely move as the last of her climax subsided.

Still kneeling, Max withdrew his fingers as he stared up at her. His pale eyes flashed with hunger as he slid his fingers into his mouth, licking them clean. Despite what they'd just shared she felt her face flame at the erotic action.

She reached for his face, cupping his cheek and jaw, needing to touch him. To her surprise, he leaned into her touch, rubbing against her. Her heart squeezed at the sweet show of tenderness. His stubble was rough against her palm and she savored the sensation of stroking his face.

Though she wanted to take off his boxers, she was afraid he'd stop her again. Before she could decide if she wanted to try, he blindly reached for the shower handle and turned it off.

When the water stopped flowing, the only sound left was their erratic breathing. Max moved with supernatural speed, scooping her off her feet and into his arms, cradling her against his bare chest. She savored the feel of his skin against hers, the strength he radiated, as she wrapped an arm around his neck.

He nuzzled the sensitive spot behind her ear as he wordlessly stepped from the shower. They were soaking and dripping everywhere but he didn't seem to notice and she didn't care. She just hoped he would let her strip off those boxers once they made it to a bed because there was no way they were done for the night.

CHAPTER FIVE

Bypassing the guest room, Max strode down the hall to his room with Lauren in his arms. He wanted her scent all over his sheets, his room, and him. Everyone would be able to scent her on him and know he was taken. Max laid Lauren out on his king-sized bed, savoring the sight of her there.

Petite and lean with a perfectly bronzed body, he wanted to kiss every inch of her. After feeling her come on his fingers and tongue, he wanted to experience her coming around his cock, to feel her tightening and climaxing around him as she shouted his name. And he wanted to bury himself balls deep inside her, pumping into her until he was completely sated. He could barely think as he stripped his boxers off.

Blindly he threw them through the open door of his bathroom. He heard them land with a wet smack against the tile before he knelt on the end of the bed. Light from the slightly parted window blinds was their only illumination. Not that he needed it with his supernatural eyesight, but with the moonlight bathing her in a soft glow, she looked like a goddess stretched out for him to feast on.

"You waiting for a written invitation, wolf?" she practically purred, her dark eyes flashing to her jaguar for a moment before turning back.

Not trusting his voice, he let out a low growl. His cock felt like a club between his legs. He ached to completely claim her even if that was way too soon. He couldn't bite her, marking her for all to know she was his, but he wanted his scent all over her, his cock buried deep inside her. It was a primal need to imprint her with his scent.

He wanted her to be branded by him, to know she belonged to him. And vice versa. He wanted Lauren's scent deep in his skin so that all he smelled was her. This wasn't just the most intense attraction he'd ever felt. It was the mating call.

He knew it in a bone deep way and accepted it. He didn't care if she was a jaguar and he was a wolf. It was uncommon in the shifter world for different species to mate, but they could make this work. Yeah, they needed to get to know each other a hell of a lot better, but his wolf had already accepted her. On the most primal level possible, his animal knew what he wanted and would accept no other female. That was the most important thing.

As he started to crawl up the bed, a predator intent on claiming his prey, Lauren let her thighs fall open, exposing her mound and that delicious amber and vanilla scent. The soft hair on her pussy was a shade darker than the hair on her head and was trimmed into a perfect little strip. He was tempted to taste her again, but right now he needed inside her like he needed his next breath. The thought of feeling her tight sheath clenching around him made him shudder in anticipation.

When he settled between her legs and dragged one finger down the length of her wet slit, she shuddered and arched her back. Pushing his finger inside her, he closed his eyes when he felt how wet she was. This was going to be heaven.

Bang, bang, bang.

His eyes flew open and Lauren straightened, inadvertently pulling away from him when she sat up. Someone was pounding against his front door. For the most part these condos had extra insulation because of their sensitive hearing and all the front doors were steel reinforced. Whoever was pounding wasn't taking no for an answer.

"It's almost four in the morning," Lauren murmured as she brought her knees up to her chest and wrapped her arms around them. "Is that normal?"

Frowning, Max shook his head. "No." Most of his pack members would just call if there was an issue. Annoyance settled over him. Ever since Grant had left, it was like half the pack had forgotten how to take care of their own problems. Either that or Grant dealt with more than Max had ever realized.

Max grabbed a pair of boxers from one of his dresser drawers and tried to will his cock to go down. "I'll be right back. Someone better be dead or dying," he muttered as he left.

He could hear the sheets rustle as Lauren got out of his bed, but he hurried down the hall as the incessant banging continued. When he neared the front door he scented four different packmates, including a male he didn't care for. Max immediately tensed. For the most part he got along with everyone in his pack, but Wade Burks was a pain in the ass. Grant had taken him and his sister in about two years ago and the guy just rubbed Max the wrong way. There better be a damn good reason for him to be at his place this early in the morning, especially because they'd just interrupted him and Lauren.

Taking a deep breath, he pulled the door open to find Wade, his sister Naomi, and Sapphire and Charlie from the bar standing there. Still wearing the same clothes they'd had on earlier, Sapphire and Charlie looked grim, but Wade and his sister just looked pissed.

"What's going on?" Max asked, keeping his voice as calm as possible. Whatever it was, it was clear he'd need a level head.

"Your bitch robbed us," Wade growled.

Max didn't even realize he'd reacted until his fist connected with Wade's face. The crunch of the other shifter's nose breaking against his hand was a jolt to Max's system. With an enraged snarl Wade flew back through the air and slammed against the outer hallway wall.

He pushed up but before he could make a move toward Max, Charlie smoothly stepped in between them. "I think what Wade means is that while he and Naomi were watching Grant's house, *someone* slipped in and tripped the silent alarm on the safe. Now the brooch is missing."

"Well it wasn't Lauren." Though he was still raging inside, Max kept his wolf in check. He could scent and hear Lauren behind him. Sure she'd been with him, but he knew she wouldn't have done this.

She had no reason to since she was getting the jewels in a week. But it was more than that. Her quick offer to help out at the bar had been so selfless and he knew it was because she'd been feeling guilt over breaking in to Grant's place. She wanted those jewels for her sister and he understood wanting to look out for family.

"I'm sure it wasn't, but maybe one of her pridemates is behind this?" Naomi asked, her voice even, unlike her hostile brother. She looked angry but was at least acting civil. Her eyes narrowed a fraction as they landed somewhere behind him.

Lauren strode up wearing one of his T-shirts and a pair of his sweatpants. Both were too big on her, but she looked…adorable. And he liked seeing her in his clothes, being covered by his scent. With her, she brought the scent of sex, something the others wouldn't be able to miss. Whatever anyone had thought about her staying under his roof and then his display of aggression at the bar, now it was confirmed that they were sleeping together. Or they would be soon.

Max reached out to wrap his arm around Lauren's shoulders, a silent claiming his packmates couldn't misunderstand. She stepped into his embrace, sliding her arm around his waist, but didn't look at him. She pinned Naomi with a hard stare. "What's this crap about my pridemates being behind something?" It didn't matter that she was nearly a foot shorter than the woman, Lauren looked and sounded intimidating.

Naomi held up her hands and shrugged as Wade growled curses under his breath. Before either could speak, Charlie interjected again, always the voice of reason. "As you know, they were guarding the house tonight."

"Not very well," Max growled. After the incident with Lauren's break-in, everyone was on rotation to guard the alpha's house. They normally had patrols anyway, but he'd stationed packmates in the house. "And why are you and Sapphire here?"

Charlie shrugged. "We were on our way back from the bar when we saw them heading over here. Thought we'd tag along."

Max's gaze narrowed on Wade. "Who's watching Grant's house now?"

Wade paled slightly. "Well, no one."

Max gritted his teeth and forced himself not to lash out at their stupidity. He needed facts before he could react. "First, what was taken from the safe?"

"*Just* the brooch," Naomi said, her voice almost smug as she shot Lauren a look.

"Did you at least close the safe before coming over here?"

Wade let out a low growl. "Yes."

Max scrubbed a hand over his face. That safe was state of the art with multiple sensors and a backup alarm trigger. And it wasn't visible unless you knew where to look. It wasn't as if the pack kept everything in there. Hell no. Everyone safeguarded their own valuables however they saw fit whether by keeping them in a bank or in their home, but Grant kept some of their pricier belongings close by. "I need to check out the scene." So he could pick up whatever scent was left over. Max was damn good at tracking and he just hoped he didn't scent any of Lauren's pridemates. "You two are coming with me because I want to hear exactly how you missed someone breaking into the house," he said pointedly to Wade and Naomi.

"I'll tell you how. Her pridemates—"

"My pridemates didn't do anything, you liar." Lauren growled low in her throat and Max could feel her trying to control her temper.

Max squeezed her shoulder and nodded at Charlie and Sapphire. "I want you two to stand guard out here, but give me a second." Without waiting for a response, he shut the door so he could have some privacy with Lauren.

The second it closed, she whirled on him. "I didn't do anything. I've been with you the whole time."

"I *know*." He didn't doubt that for a second. But her pride was a different story. "Is it possible one of your pridemates did this?"

She blinked, her dark eyes stunned and...hurt. The sight of that sliced through him. "Are you seriously asking me that?"

"I have to look at every angle." And he hated that he did.

"I told you they've left the area. I've talked to my cousins about this—twice—and they would never betray me. Not when I'm basically in enemy territory."

"Enemy territory?" he growled, not liking the sound of that. He didn't care if wolves and jaguars were technically enemies—or that Lauren was *technically* Max's prisoner. He wasn't her enemy.

"You know what I mean!"

Yeah, he knew. Still, it was possible someone had acted rashly. Max didn't know her pridemates.

As if she read his train of thought, she glared. "They would never take them. Not when it would be leaving me to fend for myself." Her gaze completely shuttered then. "Go look at the crime scene. Just don't expect me to be in your bed when you get back. I'll be in the guest room, as your prisoner." At that, she turned on her heel and strode down the hall with her head held high.

Max wanted to go after her, to iron all this out, but he didn't have time. If those two idiots hadn't left the house unguarded he could, but right now he needed to make sure nothing else of value was taken from their pack and to catch the scent trail before it went cold.

Letting out a savage curse, he followed after her, but only to throw clothes on. True to her word, she headed to the guestroom and shut the door behind her. He heard the lock click before he stalked to his bedroom and quickly dressed. Even though he wanted to stay and talk with her, he didn't have the luxury of time. Forcing his expression to remain blank, he opened the front door and slammed it shut behind him. Okay, the slam was childish, he just didn't care. "Let's go," he ordered, not waiting to see if they followed.

Right now he should be balls deep inside the sexiest woman he'd ever met. Not dealing with the incompetence of two of his packmates. He was seriously counting down the days until Grant returned from his honeymoon. Sometimes being second-in-command sucked.

CHAPTER SIX

Max stood in the middle of Grant's office, visually scanning the nearly undisturbed room while he tried to decipher the various scents. Grant's scent was embedded in the room and his mate, Talia's scent, was faint. He could still smell Lauren too, but it was faded, not recent. And it was very faint. Other than those and Wade and Naomi's nothing else was strong enough to stand out.

Pivoting to face brother and sister hovering outside the doorway, he pinned them with a hard stare. "Explain again how you two allowed this to happen." What good was having patrols or security if they did a half-ass job?

The tall blonds both looked embarrassed, but Wade covered it first with annoyance. "I was downstairs grabbing some food and Naomi was supposed to be upstairs covering me."

Way to throw your sister under the bus, asshole. Max had already heard their explanation but he turned to look at Naomi because he wanted to hear it again.

She glared at her brother and shrugged, as if it wasn't a big deal, which just pissed him off. "I had to use the bathroom then I smelled the barbeque downstairs. I got hungry."

"I saw the flashing green lights first," Wade muttered.

Max had made them repeat their story a few times and it didn't sound rehearsed. Whoever had managed to open the safe set off the interior tripwire, which triggered bright flashing green lights from three overhead sources within the house. They were silent but damn bright.

"I don't see what the big deal is. You know that jaguar shifter took the brooch. Punish her and *make* her tell you where it is." Naomi flipped her long, blond ponytail over one shoulder. There was a bite of censure in the wolf's words. As if she was reprimanding Max.

Her words were like pouring gasoline on the slow burning coals of his anger. Slowly, he took a step forward, his gaze fixed on her. "You were given an order and failed to follow through. That, I could deal with, if it was an honest mistake. But you're not even sorry about it. Now you want to *order* me what to do?" There was a very specific hierarchy in each pack and while the Kincaid pack rarely had problems, these were two betas in front of him. And they weren't acting like it. It rubbed his wolf the wrong way, making him edgy. Max growled low in his throat and flashed his canines.

Immediately both of them dropped their heads in submission but Wade didn't cover the way he clenched his fists into tight balls. Yeah, Max had a feeling they were going to come to blows again really soon. Since he had to cover every angle of the missing jewels, he would. And he didn't care if he pissed these two off in the process.

"You two are going to stay here until Sapphire and Charlie arrive," Max said as he pulled his cell phone out of his pocket. He hated calling them over here right now, but he knew they were still awake and he needed someone with knowledge of the situation. "While they're watching you I'm going to tear apart your place. For all I know you took the fucking jewels." He didn't know if he believed it, but he didn't like their story or attitudes and there was no way Lauren was behind this. If she said her pride wasn't either, then he had to believe her.

Both their heads jerked up at that, shock clear on their faces.

"You can't be serious," Wade snapped.

In response, Max tilted his head in the direction of the stairs. "Downstairs, now."

Glaring at him, they did as he ordered. Once they were gone, he called Charlie then did another sweep of the room and windowsill while waiting for Wade and Naomi's babysitters to arrive.

* * *

Lauren glanced at her cell phone as it rang for the third time. Max again. She silenced the ringing.

Not only had he insinuated that her pridemates might be behind this, but he'd left two of his packmates to watch her. Like what, he thought she'd leave? She'd made a deal with him and after what they'd just shared she expected…hell, maybe she shouldn't have expected anything. She actually understood that he needed to investigate every angle and if that included her pride, fine. But he'd left two shifters to watch her. Because he didn't trust her.

That hurt.

Rolling over, she stared at the ceiling, hating the conflicting feelings surging through her. She was more attracted to Max than she'd ever imagined possible. The man was sexy and infuriating and from what she'd experienced very giving in the bedroom. Sure they hadn't actually had sex yet, but he'd already proved how much he wanted to please her. And she wanted to do the same, to lick and kiss every inch of his delectable body.

But there was more to any relationship than the physical stuff. She'd be leaving soon anyway so why was she thinking in 'relationship' terms. Groaning at herself, she grabbed a pillow and held it over her face while she screamed in frustration. The run from the bar to Max's condo had been too short to relieve her tension. Now she was even more wound up with sexual frustration. It didn't matter that she'd had an orgasm. That had barely taken off the edge of her hunger.

She'd seen that look in Max's eyes and she'd been primed for him to thrust inside her, to fill her until they were both boneless from pleasure.

When her phone started ringing again she snatched it up, but frowned when she saw her cousin's name on the caller ID. About an hour had passed since Max had left but it was still early. She answered immediately. "Hey, Yelena. Everything okay?"

"Um...not exactly."

Oh, crap. Lauren knew exactly what her cousin was going to say before the words were out of her mouth. There was no other reason for her cousin to be calling. "He knows." He, meaning her father.

Yelena cleared her throat. "Well, yeah."

"Is he pissed?"

"I don't know."

Lauren blinked. "What?" How could she not know?

"One of the aunts overheard my bigmouthed little brother talking about you and apparently told your mom—who is super angry. But your dad hasn't said a word to any of us and he knows we're involved. He hasn't called us to his home to yell at us, nothing. It's weird," she whispered the last part, as if afraid of being overheard.

It wasn't weird. When their alpha was truly angry he contained his anger until he'd moved past his initial period of rage. He was her father so she knew better than most. He was a good alpha and never wanted to lash out at those he cared about so he waited until his animal was under control. And right now he had to be crazy angry. Lauren was the baby of the family. It didn't matter that she was twenty-five. Her older sisters were all over a hundred and her parents were over three hundred years old. She'd been a surprise. Her whole family had practically smothered her in their over protective tendencies.

Oh yeah, she knew what was coming. "I've gotta go." She hung up without waiting for a response, not caring if it was rude. Her father was either about to leave for Gulf Shores or had already left. He wouldn't have told her cousin or anyone else involved. Nope, they would have been able to warn her and he wouldn't want that.

A rush of adrenaline punched through her as she threw off the covers. Stripping off Max's clothes, she hurried to the shower. The surge of cold water blasted her, but she welcomed it. Right now she needed to get as much of Max's scent off her as possible. Not because she was embarrassed by their relationship, but because she didn't want her father to go insane before she'd managed to explain all the details.

Once she'd changed into her own clothes and pulled her damp hair up into a ponytail she snagged her phone from the dresser. She called Max as she headed for the front door. Pulling it open, she was surprised to find no one there.

And of course Max wasn't answering her call. It actually just went straight to voicemail so she texted him. Frustrated, she shoved the phone into the front pocket of her jeans and headed for the front door. Taking a deep breath, she opened the door and waited to be stopped by her babysitters.

Neither Charlie nor Sapphire were there.

Not going to waste time questioning the fates and her good luck, she hurried toward the elevators. Since he had the penthouse there weren't any other pack members on this floor. She'd met enough of them yesterday that she felt comfortable asking around.

She just hoped word hadn't spread that she or one of her pridemates had stolen that brooch. Considering the way the pack had given her a chance even after she'd tried to steal from them, she wasn't sure what her reception would be. But she had to let Max know her father was on his way. Or at least knew about what she'd done. Max had made the assumption her parents knew about her covert retrieval attempt and she hadn't corrected him. The last thing she wanted was for him to be blindsided. She knew how quickly things could get out of control when tempers were high. Especially between two alpha males. Max might not be alpha of his pack but he was second-in-command for a reason.

Lawrence Hayes was one scary alpha when he wanted to be. And her father would strike first and ask questions later if he thought something had happened to her.

Lauren rode the elevator down to the third floor. She'd borrowed potatoes from a sweet wolf shifter about two hundred years old yesterday and hoped the woman knew something about Max. She felt bad because it was fairly early but hoped the woman wouldn't mind.

Her ballet-slipper type shoes were silent against the hardwood floors as she made her way down the hallway. Instead of leaving the hallways open like so many condos on the beach, they'd glassed everything in giving them more privacy and eliminating much of the outside sound. She couldn't be sure but she guessed it was reinforced or hurricane resistant type glass.

As she neared the end of the hallway an unfamiliar, almost chemical scent tickled her nose. It made all the hair on the back of her neck stand up. Feeling as if she was being watched, she started to turn around when something slammed into her shoulder blade.

A sharp, piercing pain quickly followed, spreading out to all her nerve endings. Feeling almost numb, she instinctively reached around to where the pain was the worst. Her fingers brushed something embedded in her skin. Crying out, she pulled on it as she turned and stumbled. Blinking, she realized she held a dart in her hand.

What the hell?

Why would someone shoot her with a dart? Falling to her knees, she struggled to keep her eyes open. A dark, blurred figure was advancing on her. She tried to focus but it was impossible. The dart fell from her limp fingers, but somehow she drew on the strength to undergo the change. If someone wanted to hurt her, it would be a hell of a lot harder with her in her jaguar form.

Losing consciousness, she gave into her animal, letting her jaguar take over, protect her. She was vaguely aware of the sound of clothes shredding and ripping as her bones broke and realigned before complete darkness engulfed her.

CHAPTER SEVEN

Max looked around his guestroom, his heart thumping wildly against his chest. After searching Wade and Naomi's place—and coming up empty—he'd received a text from Lauren telling him to call asap. She might have called too, but he didn't always get service in the condos so he couldn't be sure since a missed call wouldn't have shown up. He wished he knew how long ago the text had been sent. He'd received it the moment he stepped out of Wade and Naomi's place but she could have sent it much earlier when he wasn't receiving a signal. Since then he'd tried calling half a dozen times but she hadn't responded.

He'd tried to brush it off, but standing in his condo now…he was worried. Her phone was gone but all her clothes were still there. If she'd planned to leave she would have taken everything with her. At least that's what his gut told him.

Lauren wasn't a coward. She wouldn't just run because of their sort-of argument. And not because she still wanted the jewels. Even though they were still getting to know one another something told him she was the type of woman to stay and fight and honor the terms of their initial agreement. If she was pissed about something she'd yell at him before she'd tuck tail and run.

Now he just wished he hadn't called Sapphire and Charlie to watch their alpha's place, leaving Lauren unguarded. He hadn't truly thought Lauren would leave, but he'd had to show his packmates that he was following all standard procedures of an investigation.

Keeping his cell phone in his hand, he headed out of his condo. Her scent trail was so damn faint he could barely smell it. Unlike most shifters, hers faded right away, making it difficult to track her. It wasn't as if she was covering her scent with perfumes or anything either. It simply faded.

Something about that bothered him but he didn't have time to dwell on the reasons behind it. He followed the trail to the elevators then stopped on each floor until he picked it up again. At the third floor he smelled her along with some of his other packmates' scents. But there was something else in the air too.

It was manmade, a strange chemical scent. It was so subtle he barely picked it up, but he was a damn good hunter. As he scanned the quiet hallway, he frowned at a strip of red cloth lying inside a potted plant outside of Margery's place. The two-hundred year old shifter was like a mother to Max. Hell, to half the pack. Maybe Lauren had come to see her. She'd mentioned that she'd made friends with some of the females of his pack.

Holding the cloth up to his nose, he inhaled. It was definitely Lauren's distinctive amber and vanilla scent. And he recognized the color from a sweater he'd seen among her clothes. Without going back and checking his condo he couldn't be sure if the piece of clothing was missing, but if this was hers, there weren't many reasons for it to be here. Unless she'd shifted to her animal form and shredded her clothing.

But why would she do that?

Unable to shake his uneasy feeling, he knocked on Margery's door a couple times. When no one answered, he tried again, harder this time.

When he stopped he could faintly hear her muttered 'hold your horses'. A few moments later she answered the door, her dark eyes bleary with sleep. Even though she was a couple hundred years old she looked barely thirty-five. She was tall, leggy and wore a long T-shirt that almost grazed her knees.

Considering most shifters preferred to sleep nude, she'd probably just thrown it on. She was clearly surprised to see him.

"What's going on?" she asked, her voice raspy with sleep.

"Have you seen Lauren today?"

Margery shook her head. "No, why? Don't tell me you let that girl get away. She'll make a fine mate for you."

Stunned, Max blinked at Margery's words. It wasn't that he was blindsided by the thought of wanting to mate Lauren. But how did Margery know how he felt?

As if she read his mind, or more likely his expression, her lips pulled into a thin line. "I heard what you did at the bar, getting all dominant in front of everyone. And I also remember what a monster you were after her and her pride left months ago. It didn't take a genius to figure out why you were such a bear to everyone. I'm just surprised you didn't chase after her then."

He'd gone to see her, or tried to, but no one needed to know that. Right after he'd decided to hunt Lauren down he'd received word that his mother had died. Shifters lived a long time but they weren't immortal. And his mom had been killed by a rogue vampire. Considering his mother had chosen to live alone with her mate in the mountains instead of a pack, they'd been ripe for any predators to pick off. Max had taken time away from his own pack to hunt down those vampires and by the time he'd returned to his own pack, he'd been in no frame of mind to court someone. Which was what he'd planned to do with Lauren. He'd needed a couple months to get his shit together before going to see his future mate. But now wasn't the time to focus on any of that.

He needed to find his female and didn't want to open up a conversation on his feelings or intentions with Lauren when he didn't even know if she'd left him or where she was. "If you see her, call me." Without waiting for a response he headed for the stairs instead of the elevator. He heard Margery grumbling something under her breath behind him, but he didn't care.

As he pushed the door to the stairs open, his cell phone buzzed in his hand. Jumping like a randy cub, his short-lived burst of hope that it was Lauren fizzled when he saw Derrick's number. "Yeah?" he growled into the phone.

"We've got a problem. Lawrence Hayes is at the gate with his mate and four males and they look ready to storm the place. He wants Lauren." Derrick's voice was hushed, as if he didn't want to be overheard.

Shit. "I'll be down in a few seconds." Max was already racing down the stairs as he spoke. He'd been more than surprised Lauren's pride had sent her here—or at least been okay with it—and that they'd let her stay for a week without an argument. She said she'd convinced them she was safe and he'd just been so damn grateful to have her under his roof that he hadn't pressed her for details. If Lawrence Hayes was here, that meant trouble. The male had three older daughters yet he'd named Lauren after him. She was the baby of his pride, basically a princess to the male.

And she was missing.

As Max ran, he scented Lauren and that chemical stench in the stairwell, all the way down until he reached the bottom stair. Once outside it seemed to scatter in different directions. His wolf was agitated, scratching at him, telling him find her *now*.

Before he raced off without having a clue which direction she'd gone in, he needed to talk to her father. If he didn't, things could get volatile and no one wanted that. He kept up his quick pace as he headed across the pavement. Their condominium only had one main gated entrance for vehicles. Everything else, including the parking lot was walled in. They'd added some extra security when they bought the place so they could maintain privacy from prying human eyes.

But a wall and a gate weren't going to keep out the Hayes pride.

Max slowed as he neared Derrick and five of his own packmates standing with aggressive postures near the main gate. Behind it, two luxury sedans were parked, the engines off. And next to the vehicles were Lauren's parents and pridemates.

Tall and muscular with blond hair, Lawrence Hayes was classically handsome. His wife stood next to him, the petite dark-haired female looking a hell of a lot more scary than her mate. Her claws were unsheathed and her jaguar was clear in her eyes. She was barely containing her cat. Even with their angry expressions, Max could see where Lauren had gotten her looks. She was the perfect mix of both her parents.

Her very angry parents.

"Where is my daughter, wolf?" Dominga Hayes snarled, taking a menacing step toward him.

Before Max could respond, Lawrence placed a calming hand on his mate's arm. "We've heard what

Lauren did and while this was not something our pride condoned, we've come to make compensation. She is young and foolish, but she should not be held prisoner for a mistake. I take full responsibility for my daughter's actions."

Though he looked fierce and intimidating standing there, Max could see the fear bleeding into Lawrence's gaze. He was afraid for his daughter and was trying to remain civil.

Max wondered how much they knew just as he realized there was a lot he needed to explain—like the deal he'd made with Lauren. Because clearly her parents hadn't even known she was here. But at the moment, there wasn't time for in-depth explanations. Only quick, cold facts. "Lauren has not been harmed nor will she be. Ever. She's going to be my mate if she'll have me."

There were gasps of surprise and disbelief from the jaguars, but not a sound from his packmates behind him. Yeah, word would have spread by now just how serious he was about Lauren. Before they could respond, he continued. "We had a break-in at our alpha's place a few hours ago. While I was investigating, Lauren...disappeared. I can't find her, but I followed her scent trail as far as I could go. You can ask all the questions you want or rip me to shreds *later*. Now, we need to find her." He looked over his shoulder at Derrick. "Open the gate."

At his command, the iron gate began to roll back until nothing separated them.

Worry was clear on both her parent's faces and he could see the restrained violence lurking in Lawrence's gaze. Not to mention all the questions. Stepping ahead of his pridemates and into the wolf den, Lawrence gave him a hard stare. "You and I will speak soon. Now where did you lose the scent trail?"

Though panic was still a live wire humming through him, Max was thankful Lauren's pride was willing to work with them instead of wasting precious seconds fighting or demanding answers. However, he knew that veneer of civility would be stripped the moment Lauren was found.

And he didn't care. As long as they found her unhurt and alive, he could deal with anything. Including the wrath of her entire pride.

CHAPTER EIGHT

Lauren opened her eyes and shifted against…a sand covered wood floor. Blinking into the dimness, she shook her head and realized she was in her jaguar form. Her surroundings were much clearer and focused than when she was in human form. As soon as that knowledge slammed into her, so did her last memories and she went completely immobile in case she wasn't alone.

That chemical scent, then someone shooting her with a dart. She didn't remember much after that other than her hard shift to her jaguar form. Her animal had taken over, wanting to protect her. She wasn't in pain and it didn't feel as if anything was broken, but she couldn't be sure until she moved.

Slowly, Lauren glanced around and realized she was in a shack or house of some sort. Ocean waves crashed nearby so she was close to the beach. Pushing up on all fours, she turned in a circle. She was in a room with a dingy old mattress and two boarded up windows. The door was shut though she didn't hear any sounds of life on the other side.

Since her choice was to bash the door down with her large frame or shift back to human and open it up, she underwent the change.

Biting back a cry of discomfort, she let the shift flow through her. Her bones altered, broke and realigned as skin replaced fur. Crouching low, it took a moment for her surroundings to come in to focus again. She tried to keep her breathing as steady as possible in case anyone was nearby, but couldn't stop taking deep breaths. The oxygen invading her lungs helped clear her head, though she was still feeling unsteady and had a pounding headache.

She was much stronger and more resilient than humans but she had no clue who had taken her or what they wanted from her. It was obvious they'd drugged her and she needed to find out the purpose. She also needed to find out how much time had passed.

After listening for another full minute and hearing only silence, Lauren pulled the door open. It emptied into a quiet hallway. More wood floors, more sand and graffiti on the walls. She scented old food…pizza maybe, somewhere in the house. She stepped over empty beer and soda cans as she headed down the hallway of what she now guessed was an abandoned house.

The hallway emptied out into a living room with even more beer cans and half a dozen crates that created a circle. There were ashtrays next to the crates and the lingering scent of weed filled the air. She might be wrong, but something told her that this was where teenagers or college kids hung out. Earlier last week when she'd done reconnaissance of Gulf Shores she'd seen a few abandoned homes along the beach and she wondered if she'd been taken to one of them. Hell, she wondered if she was still even in Gulf Shores.

The tang of salt in the air and sound of waves was stronger now. Light filtered through two boarded up windows so she knew it was day time, but she didn't bother with the boards. Even though she was naked, she had to get out of here and figure out where she was. She strode right for the door. When she didn't hear any human sounds or anything else out of the ordinary, she pulled it open a fraction.

A back porch led right to a sandy incline that connected to a long deck. Though she couldn't see the ocean because of sand dunes, she could hear it more clearly now. Along with very faint voices and laughter nearby. The sun was bright and high in the sky with no clouds in sight, which told her she'd been taken at least a few hours ago. Unless this was the next day. Taking a chance, she stepped outside. A gust of wind rolled over her naked body, but she ignored the discomfort.

Right now she needed to find clothes, then find a phone to contact Max. Two easy goals.

Then she was going to find whoever had drugged her and dumped her here—wherever here was. And she was going to get some answers.

To her right was a boarded up two-story home. Maybe they'd been hit with hurricane damage and never repaired. She didn't really care, she just needed some clothes before a human saw her and freaked out.

To the left of the house was a motel about fifty yards away that looked as if it hadn't been updated since the 80s. She could faintly hear people on the beach, but decided to head to the motel instead. For cover, she used the overgrown grass and weeds in the lot separating the home and the chain link fence around the motel pool.

Feeling incredibly vulnerable and exposed in her naked state, she drew on her supernatural speed and raced along the length of the fence and only stopped when she was able to hide behind the end of the motel wall. She stood on the side that faced the beach. The actual ocean was blocked by a huge sand dune and overgrown bushes. She heard a creaking sound and peered around the corner to see a maid pushing a noisy cart down the sidewalk in Lauren's direction.

The dark-haired woman stopped at one of the doors and knocked. When no one answered, she used a master keycard to enter.

Upon seeing they used keycards instead of actual keys, Lauren's heart pounded in anticipation as a plan formed in her mind. After scanning the pool and surrounding area around the motel, she decided to take a risk.

Even though she was weakened from her earlier burst of speed, she sprinted down the walkway and snagged a white towel from the cart. She quickly wrapped it around herself then stumbled into the room, forcing herself to trip over her feet as she walked.

"Cindy!" She shouted to her non-existent friend. "Where are you? I can't find my key." Lauren kept her voice loud and obnoxious as the maid's head peeked out from the bathroom door. Pretending to stumble again, she squinted as if she couldn't see straight. "Who are you?" she demanded.

The maid blinked and glanced at her towel. "Are you all right?"

"I'm...fine," she said, over pronouncing the 'n'. She moved a few steps closer. Even though the motel didn't look like much on the outside, the interior room was clean and smelled like a mix of the beach and fresh linens. "Where's my friend? I went to grab some ice and..." She looked down at herself and frowned. "I think I forgosh the bucket," she slurred, hoping she wasn't laying it on too thick.

"Hon, I think you might need to sit down. Have you been drinking?" The petite woman crossed the few feet separating them and wrapped her arm around Lauren's shoulder to steady her.

"Just a little. Thish doesn't look like our room though." Glancing around, she squinted even harder.

"What's your room number, hon?"

"Two two three." She said each word succinctly, nodding her head each time she spoke. Even though she felt like an idiot acting this way, she used her speed and stealth to snag the keycard from the woman's belt chain.

"This is one twenty three. You're on the bottom floor." The woman gave her a pitying look and Lauren popped up from her seat, giggling like a drunk

"Sorry!" she shouted again, using her 'drunk girl' voice before hurrying from the room.

Lauren could hear the woman muttering about foolish young girls as she raced back down the sidewalk. She knew she'd have to work fast before she was caught. Bypassing the room next to the one the maid was in, she kept moving until she found a room with partially open curtains three doors down. She could see a suitcase on the small round dinette table. After knocking twice, she used the keycard to slip inside.

She felt like such a jerk stealing a stranger's clothes but she couldn't run around in her jaguar form or naked. After a check of the bathroom confirmed the room was empty, she flipped up the top of the already unzipped black suitcase. T-shirts, bathing suits, jeans, shorts and long dresses filled it. Summer was over but the truly icy fall weather hadn't set in yet. Still, it was pretty cold to be at the beach. Probably a snow bird from up north taking a break from real cold weather.

In record time she threw on a blue pair of loose cotton shorts and a simple V-neck black T-shirt. The clothes were one size too big and too long for her petite frame, but they fit well enough and more importantly, she wasn't naked anymore. She also snagged a pair of flip-flops a size too big before hurrying out the way she'd come.

She practically flew down the sidewalk in the direction of the street, only stopping to drop the keycard in a bin that held mini-shampoos on the maid's cart. Next stop, finding a phone and calling Max.

Though she was tempted to go to the front desk of the motel and ask if she could use their phone, she didn't want to risk being seen by the maid or the person she'd stolen clothes from. When she reached the front parking lot of the motel she could see the other side of the turquoise and white sign that had been hidden from her before.

The phone number for the motel had the same area code as Max's number. She was *still* in Gulf Shores. Hurrying toward the main road, she paused, looking both ways and trying to find a landmark. She sucked with directions on a good day and couldn't figure out where she was since nothing looked familiar. Randomly guessing, she headed east.

Her flip-flops smacked against the sidewalk as she took in her surroundings, trying to find anything that looked familiar. It was just one motel or hotel after another. When she finally saw a pharmacy her heart rate sped up. Without cash she was pretty screwed, but there was a payphone. If anything she'd attempt to call Max collect. Now she was glad she'd memorized his number.

As she neared the store, a black sedan squealed to a stop next to her. Fearful it might be whoever had taken her, she tensed, ready to bolt when she saw her mother behind the wheel of the car.

Before she could respond, her mother leaned over lightning fast and threw the door open. "Get in."

Ah, shit. She was incredibly relieved to have been found, but still, she'd rather deal with her dad than her mom any day. A war of relief and panic waged inside her. Feeling like a twelve year old cub, she slid into the vehicle and put her seatbelt on.

Her mom didn't say a word as she pulled into the pharmacy parking lot and found a space. When the vehicle was in Park, her mom turned to look at Lauren. Worry shone bright in her dark eyes. "Are you okay?"

"Yeah, totally unharmed."

She let out a sigh of relief and tugged Lauren into her arms, which was awkward with the seatbelt. Lauren could feel tears on her neck as her mom hugged her in a death grip. Finally she pulled away and swiped at her wet cheeks. "We were ready to storm the Kincaid pack's territory but his second-in-command informed us you were missing. Where have you been? What happened? Did anyone hurt you?"

Oh, they'd met Max. And she needed to know if he was okay and where he was. "Is Max okay?"

Her mother's lips thinned. "He's fine. He's out looking for you as we speak. You shouldn't be worried about him anyway. Now tell me what happened, we've been worried sick."

Relief slammed into her that Max was unharmed and she was also warmed by the fact that he was searching for her.

Lauren took a deep breath before launching into what happened. "I was on my way to find Max when someone—in the condominium—shot me with a dart gun. I was definitely drugged but I shifted to my cat before passing out. Then I woke up in jaguar form in an abandoned house about a mile back." She motioned with her hand. "I have no clue who took me or why. I just got out of there as fast as I could in case they came back." She pressed an unsteady hand to her stomach as a wave of nausea swept through her. "I'm pretty sure there are still drugs in my system."

Dominga Hayes rubbed a hand over her face and shook her head. "You were shot with a dart gun? By one of those wolves!" She shouted the last part, anger overtaking her delicate features.

"Yes, and we need to figure out who did it." And she desperately wanted to get back to Max. She already missed his scent on her. The most primal part of her wanted to be held by him and to hold him back.

"I don't even know where to start, Lauren. You're trying to put me in an early gave, I swear. What the hell were you thinking coming here? Those jewels aren't worth your life! And now some lunatic shot you with a dart gun. If it happened in their secure condominium it had to be a wolf."

And there it was. Her mom had a wicked temper and if she hadn't been kidnapped Lauren knew her mom would have laid into her earlier than this. "Mom, I know, but—"

"No buts. We need to contact your father so we can leave. He will compensate the Kincaid pack for all their troubles and you will never come into this territory again." She started the engine as she spoke.

Yeah, that wasn't going to happen. She might have done something stupid, but she wasn't a child. And she wasn't staying away from Max. No way.

"Mom, I'm not leaving, but we'll discuss that later. First we need to find out who took me and why."

"It was one of those wolves. Who cares why? They were probably just angry a jaguar was in their territory and tried to steal from their alpha, which is all the more reason for us to get out of town as soon as possible. I want you safe. No one will ever take you again." Her hands shook as she reversed the vehicle and guilt punched into Lauren at the sight.

Her parents loved her so much and she them. She was incredibly grateful to have such a loving pride but she couldn't run away. "Mom, we can't just leave. I gave Max my word I'd stay for a week. In return he's giving us the brooch. And before you freak out, he's not actually punishing me."

"You're sleeping with him." It wasn't a question. Her jaw was set in an angry line as she pulled back onto the road and headed east.

"Not…yet." She so didn't want to talk about this with her mom. Ever. "That's not important anyway. I need to call him and tell him what happened." He would be worried and she hated the thought of causing him any kind of pain.

"I need to call your father first." Lips pulled into a thin line, her mother pulled her cell phone out of the center console. Before she could do anything, it rang.

Lauren saw her father's name on the caller ID and inwardly winced. He was going to be so disappointed in her, which sucked. It would have been one thing to come home with the brooch and deal with their annoyance but it was totally different to have them find out now.

Her mother answered immediately and the phone immediately linked up with the speaker system in the vehicle, letting Lauren hear her father's voice clearly. "Where are you?"

"I've found Lauren. She's safe and unharmed, but has some things to tell you. We're returning to the Kincaid compound," she said on a sigh, as if it was the last place she wanted to go.

"No, take her and leave."

Lauren bristled at the command. "Dad, I'm right here. We're not—"

"Some lying female is saying you attacked and tried to kill her when she caught you trying to smuggle out the jewels."

Surprise slammed into Lauren's chest as she leaned back against the seat. "What? That's not true!" And why would anyone make that claim?

"I don't care. Dominga, get her out of town now." He ended the call before either of them could respond.

Lauren turned to look at her mom, ready for an argument. There was no way she'd leave like this. She understood that her pride just wanted to protect her, but she had to iron out all this mess before it snowballed into something totally unfixable. Leaving was not the answer.

CHAPTER NINE

Max wanted to rip his hair out at the scene before him. Wade was pacing angrily in front of the floor to ceiling windows in the living room of Max's condo, his wolf clearly agitated and ready to lash out if his extended claws were any indication. But he'd been surprisingly silent as his sister shrieked and screamed.

A bloodied Naomi sat on the wood floor, crying about how Lauren had attacked her. The jaguars, minus Dominga Hayes, were all on the other side of his expansive living room glaring daggers at the blond wolf while three of his own male packmates stood defensively between Naomi and them.

The sparkling brooch was in the middle of his coffee table where Naomi had slammed it down. She swore up and down that Lauren had attacked her when Naomi caught her trying to leave the condo. Lauren had supposedly dropped the brooch then attacked Naomi and left her for dead before making her escape.

Max couldn't scent any lies coming off the blond. But his gut told him there was no way in hell Lauren had done this. Absolutely no way.

"Why would Lauren do such a thing when you'd already promised her the jewels in a week's time?" Though untamed violence rippled off Lawrence, his voice was steady as he looked at Max. He was a true alpha, a good example of what one should be like. And Max missed his own alpha more than he ever had. He'd actually called Grant a few hours ago while they were searching for Lauren, but true to his word, his alpha had turned off his phone during his honeymoon.

Lawrence continued, his voice deepening in anger. "Unless you've abused my daughter in some way?"

Max snarled, even the thought of her in pain angering him. He didn't bother answering because he didn't trust his voice. Right now he was trying to keep his shit together. Lawrence had told him Lauren was safe and out of the city, which was the only reason he was managing to control himself.

She was safe. That was what mattered. He hated that she'd left with her mother because he wanted to hold her in his arms and figure out this mess. But first he needed to calm down his two irate packmates and try to figure out why Naomi was lying. Because he had no doubt she was. Grant had taken the two wolves in because they'd been desperate and had no pack, but Max didn't *know* them and he barely tolerated Wade.

When Max, his packmates and the jaguars had been out searching for Lauren, they'd stumbled across Naomi on her way back to the condominium. Luckily tourist season was over so there hadn't been many humans about, but it still surprised him *no* humans had seen her bloodied and shredded to ribbons. That alone was hard to believe. She'd already healed from her cuts—which had definitely been made by a shifter—but hadn't cleaned up the blood yet because Max had ordered everyone to his place.

Scrubbing a hand over his face, he started to ask Lawrence to give him some privacy so he could hash this out with just his wolves when the front door opened.

He couldn't see her, but he could scent that amber and vanilla scent stronger than he ever had before. Shoving past the jaguars, he'd made it two steps down the hallway when Lauren launched herself at him. She was shaking as he held her, kicking his protectiveness into overdrive. He wanted to order everyone out and tell his pack and her pride they could deal with this mess on their own.

But as second in command, he didn't have that luxury.

Her mother was behind them, giving him a cautious stare, but he ignored her. He tuned everyone out for a few seconds as he buried his face in Lauren's neck and inhaled her sweet scent. It invaded his senses, soothing his primal beast. When he thought she'd been taken from him—he shut that thought down, not wanting his inner wolf to get even more agitated. He needed to find out where she'd been. She smelled odd, like another female.

As he started to set her on her feet, an angry shriek from behind him made his wolf go on high alert, wanting to hide Lauren from any threat.

Taking him completely off guard, Lauren shoved him hard with the kind of strength only a supernatural creature possessed. He stumbled but caught himself and turned just as Naomi launched herself in their direction. She'd jumped up and was using his loveseat as a springboard for an attack.

It registered that Lauren meant to protect him as she snarled defensively, letting her claws out.

Hell no.

Max tensed, ready to take Naomi, but before either he or Lauren could move, Wade sprung into action, tackling his sister to the ground as she screamed obscenities. The strong wolf had his sister's arms pinned behind her back, his expression a mix of worry, anger...and sadness. "Get everyone out of here, Max. Please," he gritted out as he struggled with the raging female.

The please took Max by surprise. Knowing that this situation didn't need an audience—and he could take care of both these wolves with no problem if they attacked—he looked at his own wolves and they nodded without him having to say a word. Lawrence and Dominga Hayes waited until their jaguars strode out before looking at Lauren expectantly.

"I'm staying with Max." There was no room for argument in her voice.

Max wanted to order her out with her parents because he didn't want her in harm's way, but he wouldn't embarrass her or treat her like a child. If she was going to be his mate, he wanted someone who stood next to him no matter what. He had to treat her as an equal. "She stays. We'll figure this out."

After shooting his daughter a look that promised they would talk later, Lawrence Hayes left with his wife, neither saying a word. It was as if the other shifters understood any unnecessary words would only enrage the writhing female on the ground.

Once the door shut behind them, Max looked back at Wade. "What's wrong with her?"

"Nothing is wrong with me!" Naomi screamed. "Your stupid whore had to come along and ruin everything."

"Naomi, did you steal the jewels?" Wade asked, his expression tense as he struggled with her.

Max thought about intervening, but Wade looked as if he had her under control and Max still wasn't certain what the hell was going on.

The blond wolf's body slumped, going lax as she started crying. "That bitch ruined everything. I'm tired of being at the bottom of the pack. I didn't care about that stupid human you were fucking," she spat in Max's direction, the words difficult to understand through her tears and screeching. "Then *she* came along."

Max blinked in confusion. He looked at Wade with eyebrows raised in a silent question, not wanting to anger Naomi while she was finally still and semi-calm. Her sobs were growing stronger, but at least she wasn't fighting her brother.

"She's been fixated on you the past six months. We..." Wade sighed and suddenly looked exhausted and decades older than he was. "This has happened before," he said, his voice rising above his sister's cries. "It's why we had to leave our last pack. After your mom died, she just got fixated on you, said she could help heal your pain. I truly didn't know she'd taken the jewels until she showed up bloody with the brooch and a story about Lauren attacking her. I...I've seen Naomi claw herself up before and her story didn't make sense."

"Liar!" Naomi screamed.

Wade continued as if she hadn't spoken. "A few years ago she was shot with silver by a vampire from a coven our old pack had a feud with. Some of it got into her system and while it's out now, she hasn't been the same since. She became fixated on a mated male from our former pack and tried to hurt his mate. By law they could have killed her, but let us go instead."

This was all news to Max. He wondered if Grant knew, but guessed not or he would have warned him. "Why take the jewels then?"

Wade looked down at his sister who didn't say anything, but her sniffling and crying had stopped.

When she didn't respond, Max growled low in his throat. "Explain yourself, wolf." He put all the strength and dominance of his animal in his words.

She swallowed hard, the sound audible in the big room. "I heard about how you acted with her at the bar and thought if...thought if you knew she took the jewels a second time, then attacked one of your packmates, that you'd let her go. *I'm* one of your packmates. *She's* nothing, just a stupid jaguar. But you didn't even believe me, didn't want to protect me when I told you what she'd done."

Except, Lauren hadn't actually done anything. Max glanced at Lauren who just had pity in her dark eyes, no anger. It was rare for shifters to suffer from mental instability, but if Naomi had her brain or nervous system damaged with silver in the past, it was more than possible.

"My pride knows a healer out in Nevada. He's ancient and helps all species if he can. I don't want her punished. She needs help," Lauren said softly.

Max heard Wade's sigh of relief even as Naomi shouted that she didn't need help. He didn't want to punish the female wolf either, not when she was clearly unstable. But he frowned as another thought occurred to him. "Why can't I smell her lies, Wade?"

Her brother shook his head. "Because she can't tell reality from fiction half the time. I never know when she's telling the truth because she doesn't either."

And if she didn't think she was lying, her body wouldn't produce the metallic scent. "What did you do to Lauren?" Max asked Naomi this time, his wolf clawing under the surface at the thought of his female being hurt. He wanted to ask Lauren in private but they needed answers now.

As if sensing his need for comfort, Lauren stepped even closer and wrapped her arm around his waist. He tightened his arm around her shoulders, savoring the feel of her against him. She was soft and compact, and the way she twisted against him, pressing her breasts into his side made him shudder. This was where Lauren belonged. Next to him.

For a moment Max could practically smell the defeat rolling off Naomi. "I just shot her with a tranquilizer dart. After you searched our place and told Charlie and Sapphire to take over watching Grant's house, Wade went for a run but I headed back to our place. It was just chance that I saw her and...I had to take the opportunity. It was *fate* that she was on my floor so I shot her and carried her to an abandoned house along the beach. I never planned to kill her, just prove how untrustworthy she was." Even though Naomi was still being restrained, she shrugged again in that way Max had seen her do before.

As if her actions didn't matter. As if nothing did. "You two leave now. You can pack suitcases and send for your things later, but you'll be gone in one hour. I'm spreading word to all packs I know about your sister so go see that healer if you know what's good for you. We'll get you the information, but if either of you ever set foot in Kincaid territory again, you're both dead." Max knew Grant would back him up and if for some reason he didn't, it was the only time Max would defy his alpha. If Naomi came near Lauren again, she forfeited the right to live. He had no way of knowing if she'd planned to kill Lauren or not. For all he knew, her statement about not planning to kill his future mate was another lie.

The fear he'd scented rolling off Wade lessened, but not by much as he dragged his sister to her feet. Max felt pity for the guy, but he should have come to someone in the pack before something like this happened. Especially since it had happened before.

Max swiftly moved and put his body in front of Lauren's as the two left. He knew the others outside would have heard everything and while he wanted to order one of his wolves to escort them out, this was something he had to do. For Lauren, for himself, for his pack.

He'd contact Wade later with the healer's information but first, he had to get Naomi off pack property and as far away from Lauren as possible.

Once the door shut, he turned to Lauren who immediately cupped his face in between her long, elegant fingers. Her expression was soft. "Go take care of pack business. I swear I'm unhurt. She just tranqued me. My jaguar took over and protected me."

"You'll be here when I get back?" He felt vulnerable even asking the question. Couldn't bear the thought of her leaving him now.

She smiled. "I don't care what my pride says, I'm not leaving. You and I have some unfinished business." There was a wicked note in her voice that told him exactly what she was referring to.

It relieved him, but he didn't mean short term. "This thing between us...I know we still have a lot to learn about each other, but I don't want you to leave when the week is up. Hell, I'm releasing you from your punishment. You can have the brooch now." He nodded to the table behind her. "I want you to stay because you want to."

She leaned up on her tip toes and brushed her lips against his. That one action had the ability to bring him to his knees. "I'll be here when you get back and we'll talk about the future. Go take care of pack business. I'm not going anywhere."

It wasn't exactly the answer he wanted, but it would have to do. Once he got her naked and under him, he knew he could convince her to stay long term. Sure they had a lot to discover about each other, but everything he already knew, he loved.

Crushing his mouth over hers, he kissed her hard, his tongue invaded her mouth, tasting and teasing. After he walked out that door, he wanted her to taste him for the rest of the day.

CHAPTER TEN

Max closed his condo door behind him, locking it immediately. After escorting Wade and Naomi from the property, he'd assigned two packmates to tail them out of the state. Normally he would have handled that task himself, but he needed to be with Lauren. He'd already been away from her for too long as it was. For the past couple hours he'd been dealing with the entire pack, answering questions about what had happened and why two of their packmates were now gone. No one seemed to mind that Naomi was gone, but he could tell many would miss Wade. It was a tough situation, but they were lucky to be alive. Naomi had basically attacked Max's mate. Didn't matter that it wasn't official yet, the whole pack knew what his intentions were.

He'd heard from Derrick that the jaguars had all left—minus Lauren. That news, he hadn't been expecting at all. He'd assumed he and Lawrence Hayes would be getting into it as soon as Wade and Naomi were gone.

Lauren must have been pretty damn convincing to get them to leave. He wanted to ask her how she'd managed it, but more than that, he wanted to kiss her, to mark her as his.

The need building inside him was so raw it was hard to wrap his head around it. Max stripped off his shirt as he headed for the guest bedroom, but stopped in the doorway. The bed was made and all Lauren's stuff was gone. He could still scent her, strongly, though.

In his bedroom.

He hardly remembered moving as he made his way to the end of the hallway. His throat tightened as he saw her stretched out in the middle of his giant bed, the covers kicked almost all the way to the end of it. She had a book open on her chest as she slept. Her breathing was light, barely audible—and she wore only panties. His cock instantly hardened, pressing against the zipper of his pants with insistency. Clearly she'd been waiting for him and fallen asleep.

Max didn't want to disturb her after the day she'd had. He just wanted to hold her, to comfort her. Okay, that was a lie. He still wanted to bury himself inside her, to cover her with his body and scent.

Her honey brown hair was spread out over the pillow, just begging for him to run his fingers through it. Unfortunately the hardcover book covered her nipples.

But he'd seen the light brown, tightly beaded tips and the image was seared—Lauren's eyes flew open as if she knew he was watching her.

For a moment she tensed, her entire body going bowstring tight, but then all her muscles relaxed as she stretched her arms over her head. "Hey, didn't mean to fall asleep." Her voice was raspy.

Watching her intently, Max tossed the shirt to the ground then started unbuttoning his jeans.

Lauren chuckled and sat up, but still clutched the book to her chest even as her gaze roved over his body with barely concealed need. "Not wasting any time, huh?"

"I just don't want you to be uncomfortable being the only one naked." He shucked his socks, shoes and jeans in seconds. No boxers for him. Not with Lauren around. He had a feeling he'd be going commando forever.

She snorted as he sat on the edge of the bed, but made an almost strangled sound as her gaze zeroed in on his hard length. She licked her lips and he knew it wasn't because she was trying to tease him.

Her swallow was audible as she finally met his gaze, her pupils dilated. "How did everything go?" she finally asked before glancing at the clock on his nightstand. "Did they just get out of here?"

More than a few hours had passed so he understood the question. It was already past dark. "No, they were gone within the hour, but I had to field a hundred questions from pack members about their departure, then I had to deal with regular pack stuff at one of the bars and the hotel." Max seriously wished Grant would get back to town. Being in charge was a pain in the ass. He'd never realized how whiny some of his packmates could be.

She watched him for a long moment, her eyes filled with a mix of hunger and something he couldn't define. "Do you guys have any pack owned day spas in town?"

He was confused by the change of subject, but shook his head. "Not really. There's a spa with limited amenities at the hotel, but that's it. Why?" He still sat on the edge of the mattress, his cock aching between his legs. He wanted to take her right then, but more than that he wanted to discuss what had happened and to make sure she was truly okay. And she seemed a little hesitant so he figured pouncing wasn't the smartest options.

She shrugged and after a brief hesitation tossed her book aside, drawing his gaze right to her breasts. "I've been thinking about expanding my business and opening up another location."

It was hard to focus on anything but her luscious body, but at her words he remembered she owned a high end day spa. "Where?"

She shrugged again, her mouth quirking up mischievously and his heart rate went into overdrive.

Okay, he'd go back to that later. For now, he had questions. "How'd you get your pridemates to leave?"

"It took some convincing, but after I gave them the brooch and assured them I was staying of my own free will, they had no choice to leave." Her expression was smug.

"Your father is alpha. He can do whatever he wants." His voice was wry.

"He might be alpha, but he listens to my mom…sometimes. I'm not going to lie, they're both angry at me, but I'm a grown woman. They can't force me to do anything. Even though I know they'd love to. I made it clear I was staying for a while." She looked over at the door to his walk-in closet.

For the first time he noticed it was open and all her stuff had been moved in there. Elation built inside him in a rush, the feeling almost foreign. *Lauren was staying.* That was all he and his wolf needed to know.

Hell, yeah. "So I don't have to worry about them barging in here later?"

She grinned a slow, wicked smile and leaned closer to him. The scent of her desire was potent and addicting. "Nope."

God, he wanted to cover that hot mouth with his. He slid fully on to the bed and grabbed her hips so that she had to straddle him. Letting one of his claws extend, he sliced through the delicate scrap of her panties. It didn't make a sound as the soft material fell from her body. Her thighs settled on the outside of his legs as her slick, wet opening rubbed right over his erection. This is what he'd been wanting. Still… "Are you positive you're okay with what happened?"

She pursed her lips in annoyance. "I'm fine. Yeah it sucks that a maniac drugged me, but things could have been a lot worse. No humans saw us, she didn't actually hurt me and now she's gone. And…I've got a naked, sexy man between my legs. I don't want to talk anymore."

He didn't want to either and before he could blink, her lips were on his, her mouth searching and hungry as he slid his fingers through her hair and cupped the back of her head in a tight grip. He wasn't letting this woman go. Not ever. After the way she'd tried to shove him to the side earlier, to protect *him*—nope, she was his.

They weren't done talking, not by a long shot, but she was right. They had more important things to do. Her fingers dug into his shoulders as she lifted up over him, stroking her wet slit right over him, teasing the head of his cock. He was so thankful they didn't have to use a condom. Since they were both shifters they couldn't give or receive diseases and he could scent it wasn't her fertile time. He could be inside her with no barriers.

He wanted to plunge right into her, but knew he needed to work up to it. To test her slickness first. Somehow he released his other hand from her hip and went to cup her mound but she took him totally off guard and slid right onto him with a strangled moan.

The feeling of having her tight sheath wrapped around him made his balls pull up tight and his brain short circuit. She was so *wet*. The scent of her desire was almost overpowering and he hadn't been expecting that.

"I was fantasizing about you before I fell asleep," she rasped out, her eyes heavy-lidded, the need in them clear.

He tried to make his voice work. Right now he felt like a randy cub barely able to control himself. But he wasn't going to embarrass himself before they'd even gotten started. "Don't move," he commanded, impressed that he'd found the ability to speak, though his words were more growl than anything.

Dipping his head to her breast, he kissed and licked a path around one hard nipple, never making contact with the tightened bud. Each time he got close, he withdrew, keeping his strokes light against her breast. And each time he pulled away, her inner walls tightened around his cock. Tiny little contractions that drove him crazy.

He could feel the tension humming through her as she forced herself not to move. As he'd ordered. Soon she started to rock against him, but he increased his grip on her hips.

"Tease." Her voice was urgent, shaky, and he smiled against her satiny skin.

Yes, he was. And they were only getting started. Moving with the quickness of a shifter, he repositioned their bodies so she was flat on her back with him still buried deep inside her.

Much better.

Pushing up so he was on his knees with her legs spread wide around him, he stared down at her. "Beautiful."

Her cheeks flushed at his words as she reached up to stroke her palms down his torso. Just the feel of her touching him lit him on fire and he loved seeing the hunger in her gaze. Loved seeing how much she desired him.

Her scent was enough to drive him insane but actually witnessing that hunger was erotic in a way he'd never imagined.

Reaching down, he slowly rubbed her clit as he kept his gaze on her face. Her lids grew heavy as she sucked in a quick breath. Her breathing was unsteady, but she didn't tear her eyes from his. When he removed his hand, her inner walls clenched around him and she let out an annoyed growl.

Before she could say anything, he reached up to cup one breast and said, "Touch yourself. I want to see what I missed in the shower." Ever since finding her in the shower like that, he'd wanted to actually see her doing it. He'd imagined it, but knew his fantasies would pale in comparison.

Her cheeks flushed pink again and she paused for only a second before reaching lower and pressing against her sensitive bundle of nerves with her middle finger. Watching her, he began rubbing his thumb over her hardened nipple in soft little strokes.

He studied how much pressure she used and paid attention each time her sheath tightened. The small contractions around his cock from before were growing tighter and tighter, milking him so hard he knew he was about to lose it.

But not yet.

Rolling his hips, he began moving inside her, his stomach muscles tightening as he controlled himself from coming. Her amber and vanilla scent grew stronger, headier. She was so close and he couldn't wait to push her over the edge.

He leaned down and sucked her other nipple between his teeth, hard. She cried out, her free hand sliding into his hair and gripping him with the strength of a supernatural.

"I'm close, Max."

His name on her lips—it made him absolutely crazy. He began pumping faster, her tight body welcoming him with each hard thrust. His body trembled with the need to release, the feel of her satin hold on him too much. Pleasure poured to all his nerve endings, but he restrained himself.

Barely.

Max teased her nipples with both hands and mouth as her grip on him tightened. Then he felt the trembling invade her. Her inner walls rippled around him, squeezing almost painfully as her orgasm hit.

With a soft cry, she reached around him and dug her fingers into his ass while he pumped harder and faster. He could feel the warmth of her release as her nails pricked his skin. The pleasure/pain was too much. With a growl he tore his face from her breasts, burying it against her neck as he came.

His heat flooded her as she met him stroke for stroke, her own cries of pleasure mixing with his until they both lay limp and sated for the moment. But this was just the first round and they both knew it. That had barely taken the edge off.

His cock was half-hard inside her as he raised his head to find those big brown eyes watching him with so much warmth.

"I'm glad you caught me sneaking into your alpha's house," she said softly, cupping his face with her palm.

He leaned into her hold, loving the skin to skin contact. "Me too…though I would have come for you soon anyway." It was the truth and he needed to tell her how he felt. Max didn't want any secrets between them.

Her eyebrows drew together. Sighing, Max pulled out of her, his body immediately protesting, and stretched out along her petite body, tugging her close against his chest.

Lauren immediately curved into his hold, pressing her breasts against him as she nuzzled his neck and chin. "What are you talking about?" she murmured, her breath warm against his skin.

"Six months ago, right after you left I felt…" He struggled to find the right word, but she supplied it for him.

"Lost?"

He pulled back to look at her, searching those dark eyes. What he saw floored him. It was total understanding.

"Yeah," she said, reading him perfectly. "I felt it too, but I convinced myself a wolf and jaguar had no chance at a future. That I'd worked up that weird pull in my mind, like it wasn't real."

He snorted softly at her words. "It was real all right. I would have come for you sooner, then my mom died." It was strange to admit it, but he wanted this woman to know everything about him.

Her expression softened even more. "Max, I'm so sorry."

He shook his head, not needing anyone's pity. Not that he felt that particular emotion from her. "Right after your pride left, I couldn't function for a week straight. It was like I'd gotten your scent tangled in my senses and couldn't shake it. My wolf was angry and confused when you were gone. I was ready to chase after you like a randy cub but my mom died. She was killed by rogue vamps and I had to take care of business. Her mate certainly couldn't," he spat the words, unable to hide the disgust he felt for his deceased mother's useless mate. Max blamed him for keeping his mother sequestered, living the life of lone wolves. She should have been living with a pack where she would have been protected, but there was nothing he could do about it now. "After I killed the vampires who'd attacked her, I came back here and was in no shape to court you."

Lauren smiled, at the word court, he guessed. Being so much older than her, it was a word that made sense to him, but was probably lost on her. Well, maybe not lost, but foreign. Dating was a stupid word to him though. He didn't want to fucking date her. He wanted to mate her. And courting was the only stage before that.

"I was practically crawling out of my skin the past couple months," she confessed quietly, rubbing her cheek against his chest. "Work was the only thing that kept me sane. When the opportunity to come back here to steal the jewels was brought up by one of my cousins I jumped at the chance. Not…for my sister, but because I wanted to see you again. I don't think I even admitted that to myself until just now."

Max could scent the truth rolling off her so potent it was a punch to his senses. The thought of scent triggered something else in him. "When I first scented you, you seemed surprised that I could smell you."

Lauren was silent for a long moment, her cheek resting against his upper body as she moved with the steady rise and fall of his chest. Finally she lifted her head. "I have some rare qualities and one of them is that I can cover my scent completely when I want. I have to concentrate harder than normal, but I can do it. There are only a few others like me and according to them, only their mates can scent them all the time. When I realized you could scent me, it freaked me out because you're a wolf and I'm a jaguar. My cat seemed to recognize you on a primal level but I wasn't ready to accept it. Of course you just won't take no for an answer." Her smile matched the teasing of her last statement.

"I won't. My wolf has already accepted you and the past couple days have already proved correct what my inner animal already sensed; that you're perfect for me."

"You don't care that I'm a jaguar? You realize that if—and this is a big hypothetical—we have cubs one day, we could have jaguars."

Instinctively he reached between their bodies and placed a hand over her abdomen, his fingers slightly clenching against her bare skin. "As long as they're healthy, I don't care."

Her smile grew then, transforming her entire face as she kissed him. It was a raw, primal dancing of tongues that told him they were in for a long night. The first of many. It didn't matter that they had a lot to learn about each other, they had a hell of a long time to figure everything out and Max planned to start memorizing each and every nuance of her body starting right now.

EPILOGUE

Two months later

Lauren could feel Max's gaze on her butt as she pulled another covered dish out of the oven. "You better be arranging those vegetables and not watching me," she said without turning around.

He snorted and a second later as she was placing the dish on the counter, Max was right behind her, moving with the stealth of a wolf. He nipped her ear as he slid his hands down her sides and settled on her hips, pulling her backside tight against his hardness. "I bet we have time for a—"

"You better not say quickie." Turning in his arms, she smacked him with one of her oven mitts. "This is important!"

Grinning in that wicked way she loved, he brushed his lips over hers sensually and she almost melted in his arms.

Almost.

But her parents, sisters—including her oldest sister's new mate—and Lauren's new alpha and his mate were coming for dinner. It was the holiday season, but Thanksgiving had passed a week ago. This was just about getting two alphas together—her father and her new one—and showing her new pack, which still felt weird to say since she was a jaguar, that there was no ill will between the Hayes pride and the Kincaid pack.

Ever since all that insanity with Naomi, Lauren had integrated well into the Kincaid pack. Of course Max had been the reason everything went smoothly. If anyone even thought about looking at her wrong, he growled at them in that deadly way of his. As of a week ago she'd finally got her newest day spa up and running in Gulf Shores. Most of her employees were pack members, though she had a few human hires too. Hiring packmates had been a big sign of how serious she was about staying here. Of course now that she and Max had officially mated—which was stronger than human marriages in so many ways—and his scent was embedded under her skin until one of them died, it was pretty damn clear she was staying anyway. If she even thought about the night they'd mated, with him taking her hard from behind, biting her as she came, her body turned into a quivering mess of desire.

"I know it's important," Max murmured, pulling her flush against his body as he leaned down and began nibbling on her ear. "I've just missed you all day and I can scent how much you want me."

The feel of his erection against her abdomen and the potent scent of his hunger left no doubt of that. Her nipples tightened against her bra cups and she glanced over on the wall clock. Maybe they could fit a quickie in.

"I love you so much," Max whispered against her neck and Lauren's resolve flew out the window.

Just as he knew it would. "You fight dirty." A month ago they'd both admitted they loved each other and she couldn't get enough of hearing it. Max had actually bought her flowers and a diamond ring when he told her, something out of character for the big wolf, but he was trying out what he considered human customs and Lauren found she liked them a lot. Considering his scent marked her she didn't need a ring, but she liked the extra, outward symbol of their bond. She wanted the entire world to know this male was hers. "But you're right, I think we have—"

"Lauren, we're here." Her mother's voice carried down the long hallway that led to their kitchen.

Crap, they must have opened the door without either of them realizing, which said a lot for how distracted they both were. Lauren placed a hand on Max's chest and grinned as she had to tamp down her own hunger. "Behave."

He shifted uncomfortably and let out an annoyed growl. "Fine, but after this dinner—"

"Maximus, why don't you help me with these pies and leave your mate alone for two seconds?" Laurens's mother asked as she strode into the kitchen wearing a sparkly red dress, showcasing her love of the holidays.

To Lauren's amusement, Max's ears tinged red at the use of his full name. No one ever called him that. Well, his mother had. And Lauren's mother said she was going to refer to him by his given name and that was that. He'd never argued with her.

"Hey, mom, you look pretty," Lauren said.

"Thanks sweetie, so do you. The place looks amazing." She smiled at Lauren before continuing to order Max around his own kitchen.

Lauren hid a smile at Max's embarrassment and turned back to the oven so she could pull out the remaining dish. She and Max had been working like crazy to get their house together and Lauren knew she was being a little insane about everything, but she wanted tonight to go perfectly.

Grant hadn't given her any grief about trying to steal the jewels back. If anything, he'd seemed relieved that Max had found a mate and was happy. She could see how much the alpha cared for Max and she was glad because he meant the world to her.

Max had burrowed his way into her heart and now she felt whole in a way she'd never imagined possible. She loved her mate more than anything. They'd already started bridging the gap between wolves and jaguars, with her new pack and her family's pride making an effort to get to know one another. They were small steps, but it was a start. She was looking forward to a future with Max at her side. Some days it was hard to believe she'd fallen for a wolf, but she wouldn't have it any other way.

Thank you for reading Claiming His Mate. I really hope you enjoyed it. If you don't want to miss any future releases, please feel free to join my newsletter. I only send out a newsletter for new releases or sales news. Find the signup link on my website: http://www.savannahstuartauthor.com

COMPLETE BOOKLIST

Miami Scorcher Series
Unleashed Temptation
Worth the Risk
Power Unleashed
Dangerous Craving
Desire Unleashed

Crescent Moon Series
Taming the Alpha
Claiming His Mate
Tempting His Mate
Saving His Mate

Futuristic Romance
Heated Mating
Claiming Her Warriors

Contemporary Erotic Romance
Adrianna's Cowboy
Tempting Alibi
Tempting Target
Tempting Trouble

ABOUT THE AUTHOR

Savannah Stuart is the pseudonym of *New York Times* and *USA Today* bestselling author Katie Reus. Under this name she writes slightly hotter romance than her mainstream books. Her stories still have a touch of intrigue, suspense, or the paranormal and the one thing she always includes is a happy ending. She lives in the South with her very own real life hero. In addition to writing (and reading of course!) she loves traveling with her husband.

For more information about Savannah's books please visit her website at: www.savannahstuartauthor.com.

Made in the USA
Lexington, KY
05 April 2018